D1288273

TOBIAS and the GOVERNOR

A Story of the Boy Found Living at the Governor's Mansion

Ross Malone

Cover illustrator: Katie Blake
Book design: David Ho

Printed in the United States of America

Bluebird Publishing Co.

This story is dedicated to all of the students who have visited the Governor's Mansion with me over the past forty years.

These places are important in the life of Tobias:

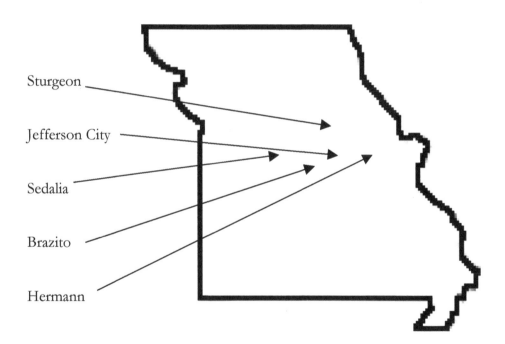

Sturgeon

Jefferson City

Sedalia

Brazito

Hermann

Contents

Fire!

Tobias awoke from a sound sleep to a clanging of bells and the sounds of shouting men. It was February but unusually warm and there had been thunder and lightening during the night. Tobias had been kept awake for much of the night by the flashes of light and then the booming thunderclaps. Once he had to move because rainwater had come dripping down from the roof of the barn right onto his cheek.

Now that the storm had passed he had settled in for a deep sleep under a thick warm blanket of straw when a clanging and shouting roused him again. He looked around to make sure that he was alone and then crept over to a nearby window. In the dim light of early morning he had trouble understanding what was happening. There was a red glow in the sky. That was normal as the sun rose in the east. But this day the red glow was coming from the west.

Tobias' head spun as he tried to make sense of what was happening in front of him. Men were running past the Governor's Mansion toward the bright red glow. Then he saw more than a dozen men in striped suits running together in the same direction. The striped clothing told Tobias that these men were prisoners from the state prison a few blocks away.

Were they escaping?

None of this made sense. Then Tobias thought that he was dreaming and all he had to do was to open his eyes, take a deep breath, and then he could go back to sleep and dream something better.

Just then a hinge creaked as a large door flew open on the front of the barn and Tobias realized that he wasn't dreaming. He ducked behind a horse stall so he wouldn't be discovered. Whatever strange thing was happening outside the barn there at the Missouri Governor's Mansion was very real. Now that Tobias was fully awake, the strange happenings were very frightening.

Two men ran into the barn and grabbed several buckets that were normally used to feed and water the horses. They also got some rope and several burlap bags. Shouting to someone outside, the two men ran out of the barn.

Tobias quickly ran back to his straw pile where he could hide himself better. He was just in time because two other men came in on the run. Tobias recognized one of the men as Paul, the stable keeper. Paul gave orders to a younger man and they quickly hitched two horses to a wagon and were gone.

When everything seemed clear and everyone was gone, Tobias carefully crawled out of the straw and made his way to the barn's door. He peeked around the corner and could see no one so he quickly and quietly stepped around the corner into the darkness. To his surprise, the side of the barn which was usually in the dark was lighted by that red glow from the west. It was then that he looked up to the west and saw it. The beautiful state capitol building was on fire!

Without even thinking about what he was doing his feet moved toward the terrible sight. The first thing he noticed was the tower of black smoke which seemed to glow red at the bottom. It looked like some strange upside-down volcano. But this one moved and grew and threw out sparks and flaming embers that were falling on houses and buildings all around. Tobias was more than a block away but he could already feel the heat of the terrible smoking red beast.

The next thing he noticed was all of the shouting. The noise drew his attention to hundreds of men running here and there in what seemed like no order at all. Now he could see small groups of women. Some merely stared at the awful sight and others were crying with quiet tearful faces that couldn't turn away from the tragedy.

He realized then that his feet were taking him closer to the horror in front of him. He kept going and felt the heat getting stronger and stronger on his face.

"YOU!" a man shouted and grabbed Tobias by the wrist. "Take these buckets! You can help!"

Tobias looked around and figured out a pattern. There were several small pumps in the area and horses were pulling barrels of water up from the river at the bottom of the hill. The men with buckets were filling them at either the pumps or the barrels and then passing the filled buckets to others who would run toward the fire and throw the water toward the burning building. He quickly took his buckets to a pump and got into the line to help pass the water along.

He could see two "pumper wagons" operated by the firemen. They were able to shoot streams of water far into the building but the streams were small and the fire was a giant. The center of the building was completely in flames but he couldn't see the far end. The east end, near Tobias, was not yet burning but the windows were broken and smoke was pouring out. The man who had grabbed Tobias's wrist yelled to all of the men, "We still have a chance to save this East Wing. Keep working, boys. Win or loose, we'll give it a good fight!"

It was then that Tobias saw an amazing sight. Paul, the Governor's stable keeper, had pulled the wagon from the barn right up close to the burning building. He was standing in front of the horses and calming them. He had covered their eyes with some sort of cloth. He stroked the animals and talked to them and they trusted Paul so much that they stood there in that heat and waited to do their job.

While Paul and the horses waited, the prisoners with the striped suits were running in and out of the burning building carrying armloads of books and papers. They would put the precious papers on Paul's wagon and then run back in for more. Tobias marveled at their bravery.

Then the wind shifted a little and the smoke moved to the south. Tobias could no longer see Paul or the prisoners. For more than an hour the buckets moved in a steady rhythm to the pumps and then to the fire and then the buckets made the same trip again and again until the men's arm's ached. More men arrived from around Jefferson City to join the fight and Tobias and some others were chosen to take a break. A man told Tobias and the others, "Take a rest for ten minutes and then replace someone else so they can rest. Good fight, men."

Tobias hadn't really thought about it until that moment. He was twelve years old and large for his age. But these men thought that he was a man also. For the first time that day a smile appeared on Tobias's sooty face. "You know," he told himself, "I've been doing a man's work all right!"
The warm feeling inside Tobias at that moment was far different than the heat of any fire.

While Tobias sat and rested he drank deeply of the water that an old man brought around to those who were resting. Then he noticed a small group of men running up the hill from the direction of the railroad station. They were dressed like firemen and carried axes, buckets, and other equipment. They were leading a team of horses which pulled a fire wagon. Someone said that these men had come all the way from Sedalia.

The first men, those who had been resting, went back to the bucket line and replaced another group so they could rest and talk about what a long fight this was going to be. But then people began talking about a water main collapse. Because of that, they said, there could never be enough water to fight the ever-growing flames. Suddenly uniformed firemen came running by yelling for everyone to move back. "She's commin' down!" they shouted. "Take your buckets!"

Everyone moved back from the fire looking over their shoulders all the while. Tobias stopped where the fireman told him to and, with everyone else, he sat down to watch and wait. At this time he noticed that there were many people standing all around. It looked like the entire city might be there watching. He saw Esther, a girl from his class at school, looking directly at him and his heart jumped for a second.

Tobias moved the buckets around in front of him so she could see that he was not a simple on-looker – he was involved in man's work. He looked back in time to see her smile at him. This man among men enjoyed that smile more than she could have known.

Tobias had never been inside the grand old building but he listened as people all around him talked about how the floors, stairways, and other parts of the building had been made of wood. They described it as a "firetrap." For more than ten years, they said people had been trying to get a new building to replace this old one. The state's voters had voted not to spend the money on a new building but Governor Hadley had been working hard to change their minds.

"Look!" someone shouted. "Look up there!" A gasp went up as the on-lookers saw the capital dome glowing bright red. As the firefighters had thrown open the doors to get in and fight and to remove precious documents, they had created an updraft which superheated the dome atop the building.

Just then a screaming roar went up from the crowd and Tobias heard what sounded like thunder in the dark sky. It was the mighty dome falling to its death. As it fell, sparks and chunks of burning wood filled the sky and showered down all around. Now Tobias knew why he was told to take his buckets. Without any orders, he quickly ran for the nearest pump and began to carry water to the thousands of little fires that were burning all around.

Several men grabbed burlap bags from a pile and soaked them till they were dripping wet. They swung these wet bags and crushed out fires at an amazing pace. Lawns in the area were burning now and the bag men were efficiently putting out the grass fires before they could grow.

The firemen had given up on the Capitol Building and were now spraying the roofs of other buildings in the area. At one point a cold steady rain began to fall and that helped to save the homes and other buildings.

In time Tobias, Paul, the firemen, the townsmen, and the prisoners had the little fires all put out but the big fire continued to burn what was left of the Capitol Building. Twice more, large sections of the building tumbled down but here and there sections of the walls stood and defied the fire to destroy them.

Pushcarts and wagons began to circulate among the men who gathered to battle the fire. They brought breakfast, water, milk and coffee from the Jefferson City restaurants. Tobias had never eaten restaurant food and he could never remember eating any food as good as this in his life. He ate a huge ham sandwich with a cup of half-coffee-half-milk and then went back for an egg sandwich with another cup of the coffee-milk.

Slowly the farmers began to leave because they had chores to do at home. Tobias knew that, if you don't milk the cows when they need it, they will "dry up" and not give milk again until a new calf is born. If the people with cows didn't milk them, there would be no milk for several months. That was also true for the people in town who kept cows.

Most of the women left and many of them came back with lemonade and coffee for the men. Tobias and the others began to walk in slow circles around the still-burning building waiting for it to burn itself out and putting an end to any fresh fires that might spring up. It was then that Tobias smiled again realizing that it was hard to tell the black men from the white men today. "We're all black when we're fighting a smoky fire," he thought. Of course he would never say such a thing out loud.

Tobias noticed that the prisoners were eating also. But they were eating by themselves, away from the crowd. The unusual thing was that Governor Hadley was talking with them. His assistant had a pad and a pencil and was writing things down as the Governor talked with the striped men. Then Tobias smiled again. The stripes were gone! They were wearing suits as black as the Governor's fine coat and trousers.

What a sight – the Governor and the prisoners, all dressed in black, drinking coffee and eating, and chatting together like old friends. It's amazing what a disaster can do to bring people together!

That evening the firemen stayed on duty but sent the rest of the men home. The police officers, the town marshals, and sheriff's deputies stayed on duty to prevent anyone from trying to take anything from the still-smoking ruins. It was still a deadly dangerous place. Tobias went down to the riverfront to try and rinse himself and his clothes off in the freezing water. The water was full of debris from the fire and not fit for cleaning anything. So Tobias went back to the Governor's barn.

There he thought of the horse trough. It was a much better place to clean up so he began with his face and arms and eventually he had cleaned all of himself and his clothing. He hung his clothing in a spot behind some lawn equipment and hoped they would dry in the cold February night air. He, with nothing to wear, slipped onto one wool horse blanket and under another then covered himself with a deep layer of straw. Tobias was so tired that he soon fell into a sound sleep and dreamed of pushcarts and wagons full of sandwiches. He dreamed of black and white people working together in a situation where you couldn't tell which was which. And, of course, he dreamed of Esther smiling at him, a man among men.

The Next Day

Long before morning Tobias was awakened by the sound of a man's voice. He opened his eyes and realized there was a lighted lantern in the barn and that Paul was putting then horses to bed for the night. He was talking to the horses as he led them to the water trough for a drink. The horses sniffed at the water but refused to drink. Paul sniffed the water himself and realized it was full of strange material and something black and sooty floated on the surface.

"Land sakes!" he said. "That smoke and soot even got in here! Amazing!"

Paul drew some fresh water in buckets and set them down in front of the horses. This they drank readily. Then he un-harnessed them, brushed them down good, and led them to their safe familiar stalls. Tobias peeked out and saw that, as Paul left the building with the lantern, he moved very slowly and looked much older than usual.

Tobias didn't remember much after that because he went immediately back to sleep. Hard work and sore muscles do that for a person. He surprised himself when he woke up early the next morning and couldn't sleep. He was so curious about what happened overnight at the fire scene and he was eager to know what adventure this day might bring.

He checked his clothing and found that it was still slightly damp but he put the cold clothing on because he couldn't wait for it to dry. He felt compelled to return to the action.

Today was not as warm as yesterday and there was a slow breeze out of the north. It came across the river and put a deeper chill into his damp clothing. Naturally the first place Tobias went for was a bonfire where several men were gathering. He stood on the warmest side of the fire and turned from time to time to encourage his clothing to dry out.

Already he could see that people were much more organized today and several men were going from place to place with pads of paper and giving orders. The firemen were busiest of all but Tobias couldn't tell exactly what they were doing right up next to the smoldering fire and rubble. To his delight and amazement two handcarts arrived where his little group was waiting and the people with the carts began to hand out thick sandwiches with eggs and cheese and a slightly tart sauce. Tobias said that he had no money to pay for a sandwich but the merchant said that the state was paying for food for all the workers. "Do me a favor," the man said. "Take two of the sandwiches and put one in your pocket for later if you want. How many coffees do you want?"

Once again, people were treating Tobias like he was a grown man. He was tall for twelve but at school everyone knew that he was just twelve. His dad probably didn't know how old Tobias was but he probably thought Tobias was younger and littler than he really was. Pap always acted like Tobias was a baby. His stomach tightened for a moment when he thought about his mother. "If she was still alive, she would know exactly how old I am," he thought. "She would be proud of me right now."

Just then a man approached Tobias's group. The man had some papers attached to a board and seemed to be giving orders. "Men! Listen to me!" he said. "First I need to see each of you and get some information. Then I'll tell you what you can do to help today. Your job will be just to pitch in as laborers and help in any way you're told to. The pay is two dollars a day, but you'll have to work hard to earn it. If you're interested, just wait until you talk to me and then we'll get down to brass tacks."

Two dollars a day! Tobias couldn't believe his ears. He had never had two dollars in his entire life. Now he could earn two dollars a day just for helping out. He would have helped out just for the excitement and, of course, for the sandwiches. He was thinking about having two dollars when he heard the man say, "You're next, son. Come over here."

"What's your name, young man?" the man asked.

Tobias stood tall and answered, "Tobias, sir."

"Tobias what?" he wanted to know.

"I don't rightly know, sir. My parents just call me Tobias and my tea... Everyone has just always called me Tobias, sir." He almost said something about his teacher. Then the man would have known that he was just a child. Tobias stood as tall as he could and decided to talk in a deep voice if he could.

"Well, you have to have a full name, son." The man continued. "Listen to me and remember this. I'm putting you down here as Tobias Joseph because, in the Bible, Tobias is related to Joseph. Now remember that. You tell the man at the end of every day that your name is Tobias Joseph and he will give you your pay."

"Thank you, sir. What man, sir?"

"Good question. Do you see those men working with the lumber over there? They're building a shack for the paymaster. He'll have the pay for you at the end of every day. Understood?"

16

"I understand, sir. Thank you very much." Tobias had that feeling again that he might just be dreaming. Two dollars a day for several days? He might be as rich as Governor Hadley before this was over.

"All right Tobias Joseph, just sign your name here and you can get to work."

Tobias signed his new name and was sent to sort through the rubbish. It was a stinky job as the fire still burned in places. He gathered rocks into one pile, bricks into another and wood went onto a series of wagons that parked beside his workplace. Nails were to be saved in a special wooden box. At the end of each day he would sort the nails into one pile if they could be used again and another pile if they were badly bent and would be melted down and made into new nails.

At noon the pushcarts came by again along with a wagon full of wooden boxes. The pushcarts brought battered and fried catfish on thick slices of fresh bread with a white sauce of some kind. Tobias had eaten catfish but never anything like this. It was wonderful! His stomach was a little upset from either the good food or from the coffee (or both) so this time he chose milk to drink with his lunch.

The men with the wagon opened the wooden boxes and began passing out leather gloves for the workers. Tobias had never owned gloves. No one in his family could afford leather gloves but now he was given a pair for free. He felt like life was getting better for him every day.

The men made a game out of yelling "Nail" every time they found one because not finding them meant that someone might step on them and that could mean dying of lockjaw. Sometimes when Tobias would yell that he found a nail some other men would yell "Good job" or "Well done, Toby."

Tobias thought that the men were just being friendly by giving him a nickname but his grandfather had been named Toby and he wouldn't let Tobias's parents name him that. Grandfather had said that "Toby" was a slave name and that his grandson should have a proper name. So the name Tobias was suggested by the A.M.E. minister and Tobias was named.

One tall soft-spoken man was named to be the foreman of Tobias's group and he came by at one time and asked Tobias if this was his first day to work here. "No, sir," Tobias told him, "I was here all day yesterday on the bucket line and putting out small fires after the building fell."

"Good enough," the foreman said. "When you check out in a few minutes, there will be two days pay for you."

Soon a loud bell began clanging and the men shouted a "Hooray" for the end of the day. Tobias had a mission so he ran faster than anyone to the paymaster's shack. "I'm Tobias Joseph, sir," he blurted out.

"Let's see now," the man said as he went down his list to the "J" names. "Yep, here we are – Tobias Joseph – two days even. There you go, son."

The paymaster only heard, "Thank you, sir!" as Tobias ran for the brick buildings two blocks over. He got there as they were preparing to close but just in time to make his purchase. He bought a new pair of bib overalls and a new blue cotton shirt. He had never had new clothing before and he felt like a king.

The store clerk noticed that Tobias's shoes were coming apart and mentioned that they had good work shoes on sale today. "That will have to wait for a day or two," Tobias answered and waited while the clerk wrapped his purchases in stiff brown paper and tied a stout string around the package.

Then he gave Tobias his twenty-eight cents change and said, "Come again."

Tobias smiled once more and said, "I believe I will."

It gets dark early in February so Tobias didn't have to wait and sneak into the barn. He just went straight to his "home" and settled in. First he took the egg and cheese sandwich out of his pocket and ate it while he thought about the twenty-eight cents in the other pocket. He discovered something then. It's hard to eat and smile a really big smile at the same time. Of course this was a whole new experience for him.

After Tobias finished his sandwich he found a small metal container which had held horse pills. He put his twenty-eight cents into the container and then buried it at the very back of the barn behind some hay bales that wouldn't be needed this year at all. "Good safe place," he told himself.

Tobias took off his dirty clothes and put on his new blue clothes. Then, instead of the horse trough, he got a bucket of water and washed the clothes he had worn every day this winter. Now they would have all day to dry and he could wear one set of clothing each day and allow the other to dry. No more damp clothing this winter!

Tobias lay down and felt the stiffness of the new clothing next to his skin. He thought about how his stomach was full of good food. Then he tried to decide what to think about next. When he fell asleep he wanted to be thinking about something great so he would have good dreams. Should he think about money in a can – or Esther's smile – or his new clothing – or tomorrow when he could buy some new warm underwear – or his mother's pride in him – or . . .?

Discovered

The next morning Tobias made certain to be at work early. He didn't want to take any chances on loosing this wonderful job. He also didn't want to miss the breakfast carts when they came by. The foreman called a meeting soon after they started. He explained that the part of the job that they had been doing would last another ten or twelve days. Then it would be time for the horse-drawn equipment and the craftsmen to come in. There might still be some jobs at that time but most of them would be laid off. As they left to go back to work, the foreman noticed Tobias with his new clothes and new gloves. He smiled and thought, "Some of these guys spent their money on whiskey. Tobias has his head on straight."

As he worked, Tobias thought. Ten more days would be twenty more dollars. With that he could buy some warm long flannel underwear, some socks and some good shoes. He would still have about fifteen dollars left over. That was more money than he ever thought he might have. So, while the other men worried and complained, Tobias thought about his good fortune.

A German restaurant supplied lunch this day and Tobias tasted bratwurst on a long split bun for the first time. He never imagined anything could be so good. But then the man with the pushcart said, "Och kinder! Here mit mustard – you see."

Tobias slathered a layer of the yellowish-gray stuff on his second bratwurst and, sure enough, it actually was even better than the first! But it did make his eyes water and his nose run just a little. He pointed to the sandwich and smiled at the old vendor. The man smiled back through his bushy beard and mustache.

After work that day, Tobias took his two dollars and went back to the store. There he purchased two sets of long flannel underwear and two pairs of tall cotton socks. The clerk wrapped them and gave Tobias his change. "See you tomorrow?" he asked.

"Soon," Tobias replied. "I'm thinking about some new shoes."

As he left the store he noticed a man walking down the street. The man stopped under a street lamp, looked at something and threw it into the trash. Out of curiosity Tobias looked into the trash and saw a copy of the day's newspaper. On the front cover was a picture of the prisoners in their striped uniforms. Tobias took the paper to see why prisoners would be on the front page of a newspaper.

That night he had no extra sandwich but he did have more money to put into the tin pill container. He also had his old clothes to put on – nice and dry. He quickly put on some new underwear and new socks then washed and hung up his new set of clothes. Putting on his old clothes, he knew that he would be very warm tonight.

That night he did something he had never done before. He was so curious about the newspaper and the stories it held that he went into a back room where Paul had a little office. There he had a lantern and a small table with a wooden chair. It was away from the outer wall of the barn so no one should be able to see a lantern turned down low.

The newspaper was fascinating. It told the story of the lightning strike that started the Capitol Building on fire. It told of all the different people who had helped in so many ways. It told of Governor Hadley and how concerned he was that someone might be hurt fighting the fires. And it told about the prisoners.

The Governor said at his meeting with the newspaper people that there were fifteen members of the prison fire brigade who fought the fire all through the day and that they also risked their lives removing priceless documents from the building. Governor Hadley said that he was recommending to the Prison Warden that he get a new fire brigade trained quickly because these fifteen men would soon be pardoned by the Governor. They were truly heroes he said and, just as they had been punished for their misdeeds, they should be rewarded for their good deeds.

"Well what do we have here?" a voice boomed in the dark night. A tall man stood in the shadowy darkness just outside the little office. Tobias had been caught.

Kindness

"Do you know what trespassing means?" the man asked.

Then Tobias recognized the voice as Paul, the Governor's stable keeper. "No, sir," Tobias replied.

"It means being somewhere where you're not supposed to be. It means that, since you're not supposed to be here right now, you're trespassing and that's a crime."

"I didn't want to do anything bad, Mr. Paul, I just didn't have any other place to be and now that the Governor has an automobile, no one uses the barn much. I truly am sorry if I did something bad."

"No, I wouldn't say 'bad'," Paul said and his voice softened. "I found some clothes hanging up to dry over there and I just wanted to see what was going on. You know, son, you really aren't supposed to be here and I will need to tell the Governor about you. I don't have any choice about that. Do you understand?"

Tobias was thinking about his job when he asked, "Governor Hadley's awfully busy right now. Do you have to tell him real soon?"

Paul laughed and said, "Clever, aren't you? Well, he is pretty busy I suppose and maybe I can wait until March when things have settled down and the weather is a little warmer. But if he asks me, I have to tell the truth – understand?"

"Yes, sir and thank you." Tobias replied.

They talked for a few minutes and then Paul left. Tobias went right to his straw pile and settled in for the night. He knew completely how lucky he was that Paul didn't turn him in right away. But Paul was true to his word and Tobias continued to work at his clean-up job for fourteen more days before the work ran out.

Two nice things happened during that time. One was that Paul would often stop by after work and see how Tobias was doing. Paul noticed that, except for the one change of clothing and some new shoes, Tobias seemed to be saving all of his hard-earned money. Paul was very impressed.

The other nice thing that happened was that, on the last day of work, the soft-spoken foreman called Tobias to the side and said, "I've noticed how you work hard all day and never complain like some of the men do. I also see that you're careful with your money and I'm very impressed with that. I just want to tell you that, if you ever need any help, you let me know and I'll do what I can. Keep your nose clean, OK?

"Yes, sir, I will. Thank you."

"One more thing," the foreman said, "When you check out at the paymaster's shack tonight, there's a dark blue winter coat hanging on the wall. It was my son's but he has another one. I'm pretty sure it will fit you so take it when you leave tonight."

Tobias didn't know what to say. He just stood there for a second with wet eyes and then he reached out and shook hands with the foreman. The foreman smiled a small smile and went about his business.

As Tobias walked to the barn that night he wore a slightly large blue coat and a wool cap that had been tucked into the pocket. He had new shoes, clothing, almost twenty-five dollars in his tin container, and a new kind of pride that he had never felt before.

The Plan

The next day Tobias was washing his clothes and thinking about where he could find some food. It was a Saturday so there was no school. Maybe he could go to the back of one of those restaurants and find something good that they might have thrown away. One thing was for sure. He wasn't going to spend any of his money until he absolutely had to.

Tobias had just finished hanging his clothes in the back of the barn when the big front door swung open and Paul walked in. He brought a huge ham and egg sandwich which he cut in half and shared with Tobias. He also offered some coffee but Tobias didn't think his stomach could handle any coffee.

The two of them sat down on some hay bales and enjoyed their sandwiches and then Paul asked, "Tobias, what are we going to do with you? Where can you live? You're a great kid and I don't want to see you get desperate and get into trouble. What are we going to do with you?"

"I don't rightly know, Mr. Paul." I can live with my Pa sometimes but then he just gets mad and blows up. I can't tell when it's gonna happen or why he does it. But he blows up and then I'm probably gonna get hurt. That's why I came here. Cause here I take care of myself and nobody is gonna hurt me – and I don't have to hurt anybody."

"Does that mean you want to hurt your father?"

"Sometimes I think about it, sir. And I even know how I could do it but I surely don't want to."

"O.K., Tobias. First, I want you to just call me Paul. Second, I don't want to see anyone get hurt either – especially a boy. How old are you anyway?"

"I'm fourteen, sir – I mean I'm fourteen, Mr. Paul – Paul."

Paul looked at the boy carefully and said, "I would have thought you were more like a big twelve-year-old."

"Well I'm almost fourteen, sir. Twelve is almost fourteen."

Paul laughed and said, "Well, it's closer than not. Closer than not. Listen, Tobias, If I'm going to be covering up for you, you must always tell me the truth. I can't be telling the Governor something and have him think that I'm a liar. Do you understand?"

"Yes, sir. I surely do. I can always go somewhere else but you can't always find another fine job like this one."

Paul thought for a minute and then said, "What I see right now is a hard-working, self-sufficient, young man with good manners and enough education that you read newspapers. What else should I know? Like where did you get your good manners and what are you long-term plans?"

Tobias answered, "I can tell you the first part. My mother always taught me that manners oil the machinery. She says manners make life easier. They're free and they buy you many things."

"Your mother sounds like a very wise woman, Tobias."

"She was, sir. She and Brother Curry over at the A.M.E. Church are the wisest people I know. That other thing you asked – about long-term plans – I don't rightly know what that means."

"It means what do you want to do with your life – you know, when you're full grown?"

"Oh that. Well my teacher wants me to go to the Lincoln Institute after I graduate from my school. She says Lincoln is like a college and I could learn a trade. But I really want to go out west like my great-aunt. I could be a ranch hand. Lots of black men are cowboys. Did you know that?"

"Yes that is true, Tobias. There's opportunity for you in the west. But there's opportunity in schooling too – even if you're a ranch hand, schooling can be very important. It's like a shield to keep the world from cheating you or hurting you. It opens doors of opportunity for you."

They sat quietly for a moment then Paul said, "A cowboy huh? That's just what I used to think I wanted to do too."

"Tobias," Paul continued, "do you go to school every day?"

"Almost every day," he replied. "Lately I've been working over where the fire was. I got paid two dollars a day! But now I'll go back to school every day but Saturday and Sunday when I go to the church."

"I suppose they give you lunch at school?"

"Yes, sir. It costs a penny a day and now I have enough money that I can pay every day. Sometimes I couldn't find a penny but they gave me lunch anyway."

"What kind of lunch can you get for a penny?"

"We get the same as every kid in Jefferson City – black or white. We get a jelly sandwich and a piece of caramel candy. I used to bring a lunch from home that my mother made for me but I can't do that any more."

At the mention of his mother, Tobias grew quiet for a few seconds then took a deep breath and continued. "You know, Mr. Paul – Paul, I have a really good teacher who does something special when the weather is cold. She starts up the stove in the morning so the room is warm when we get there. But on top of the stove she puts a pot of water and a bunch of beans. By the time we're eating lunch, the beans are ready and we get to have hot beans with our jelly sandwich. We surely do get filled to the brim on those days! That's one reason I go every single day. Besides, it's my job to put wood in the stove from time to time. I wouldn't want the fire to go cold and have everyone miss their warm cup of beans."

Paul sat up straighter and his eyes lit up. "I have an idea, Tobias. If you're going to be a ranch hand you certainly will need to know about horses, wagons, and such. Even if you change your mind about going west, it's always good to know about animals and equipment. Then you could get work on a farm, or as a stable manager for the next Governor. You know Mr. Hadley won't be here in the mansion forever."

"I know about elections, sir. But will you leave when Governor Hadley leaves?"

"Yes, Governor Hadley asked me to come with him from Jackson County and I'm looking forward to going back home some day. What do you think about my notion for you to learn about horses and such? Would you want to work with me here after school and learn about what we do? That way the Governor won't be as suspicious."

Tobias knew a good thing when he heard it so he quickly agreed to Paul's plan and he began to help with mucking the stalls and changing the bedding, currying the horses and greasing the wagon and carriages. His favorite thing was to feed the horses. They were already familiar with him but now they began to associate Tobias with food and they were "friendlier" just as they were with Paul.

The days went by and Tobias learned where a local bakery threw away their stale bread and he would stop each day and look to see if a loaf might be left. He was surprised and a little suspicious when he noticed that the stale bread started appearing outside in a clean wrapper – as if someone had put it there to be used.

After his stop at the bakery, he would hurry on home to the barn and put the bread away until after Paul had gone. At first he offered some to Paul but Paul always refused so Tobias stopped offering.

Each Sunday he would put on his newest overalls and his blue shirt and sometimes his winter coat and go to the A.M.E. Church. Everyone there called it the Quinn Chapel. After church there was always a lunch served and he got real cooked vegetables and sometimes deserts. It was his favorite time each week.

Living in a barn full of hay and straw, there is no way to have a kitchen so Tobias could never cook and he had very few opportunities to get vegetables during the cold months. In the summer he could help people in their gardens and they would pay him with potatoes, carrots, peas, green beans, berries, and other things he could eat without cooking. Even then he preferred the good cooked food at the church. One lady would sometimes bring an apple pie. She had learned how important her pie was to Tobias and she always seemed to have the biggest slice available just as he arrived at the table.

Everyone at church remembered his mother and, of course, they had all known Tobias since he was a baby. As time went by, the people at church had become a lot like some nice aunts and uncles. A few of the oldest people even remembered his grandparents and his great aunt, Cathay. Tobias always thought that, if he was ever in a real bad fix, he could count on Brother Curry, the church's minister for help. And now, he realized, he had another person he could count on – Paul.

Governor Hadley

The weeks went by and Tobias learned more and more from school and from his friend, Paul. It was now April and he never wore his winter coat. When Tobias hung it on a nail he had a mixed-up thought. "I want to get taller and stronger so I can go west," he thought, "but if I get any bigger I won't be able to wear that nice coat next year." He put his wool cap into one pocket and kept his bread in the inside pocket of the coat. He figured that barn mice wouldn't be able to climb straight up the wall and get to his bread the way they used to do.

There were fewer mice now also because a barn owl had settled in to live with Tobias. He knew that owls ate mice so Tobias never did anything to disturb the bird. Eventually a nest appeared and Tobias could hear cheeping. With the cheeping, and the snorting and pawing of the horses, the barn started to sound like a real homey place with a nice family that got along very well together.

On the evening of April 17 Tobias was brushing down one of the Governor's bay horses and telling Paul about the special Easter Sunrise Service he had attended the day before. One little boy had been told that he couldn't have communion yet because he was too young. Tobias said, "This boy said in a real loud voice, 'I want some juice and crackers too!' and everything got kind of quiet but us boys started laughing and then everybody was laughing. I don't think God would mind do you, Paul? The little sprout just didn't understand about the communion."

Paul smiled and was just starting to answer when a tall thin form appeared in the light of the doorway. "Good afternoon, Governor," they both said.

"Well, what do we have here, Paul?" the Governor asked. "Have you expanded operations and hired extra help?"

"No, sir," Paul replied. "This is my young friend, Tobias. He just offered to help out because he likes horses and wants to learn about them. He plans to go west and be a ranch hand some day. He's a good worker."

"I haven't seen anyone named Tobias on the payroll."

"No, sir. He's just volunteering and I'm trying to teach him what I know."

"Tobias," the Governor said, "if you listen and learn everything Paul can teach you, you will know far more than most men in this world."

Tobias just smiled and shook his head to acknowledge the Governor. He continued on with the horses while the Governor talked to Paul. He could plainly hear everything the Governor said.

"Paul, I have a function to attend Wednesday afternoon up at Sturgeon. I don't feel comfortable about taking the automobile that far on those roads. There will be Mrs. Hadley and myself along with two folks from Sturgeon. So I would like for you to have the large carriage ready for us right after breakfast. You know how Agnes loves to travel by carriage and she's really looking forward to this. She claims to know everyone we pass and she waves to them all. I hate to admit it but she probably does know most of them."

"I'll have everything ready for you, sir. Should I ask the kitchen staff to pack a lunch?"

"No," the Governor replied, "We'll be meeting some folks in Columbia for a late lunch. Thank you, Paul. I'll see you then."

The Governor started to leave and then turned to Tobias. "Young man, will I be seeing you on Wednesday morning also?"

"No, sir. I'll be in school on Wednesday." And then Tobias quickly added, "Unless you want me to be here, sir."

"No, son, the first answer was the best but I appreciate the second answer. School is by far the best place for any young man on a Wednesday morning. Nice to meet you, Tobias."

Governor Hadley took a quick look around the barn, then gave a little wave and walked back toward the Governor's Mansion.

Tobias relaxed and said, "He's nice."

Paul replied, "Yes, he's nice alright, and he's very intelligent. There's a lot going on in his mind and today there was something that he wasn't telling us. I know him well enough to recognize that."

The Mystery

On Wednesday morning Paul had just finished hitching the horses to the carriage and was busy wiping the brass to make the trim shine. The Governor approached still chewing the last bite of his breakfast and carrying a large mug of coffee. "Good morning, sir," Paul offered.

"And a good morning to you, Paul. Before I leave, Paul, tell me about that boy in the barn."

Paul nervously twisted his polishing cloth and said, "It's just as I told you, sir. Tobias hopes to become a ranch hand and he likes horses. I'm teaching him about the animals and the equipment. He greased the carriage for you today and I checked it – he did a good job. He's a good worker and a good kid."

"I believe every word you told me," the Governor replied. "It's the part you haven't told me that has me so curious. I saw a winter coat hanging in the barn in April. The staff tells me that they see the boy arrive after school but they never see him go home. They do, however, see him leaving the barn very early in the morning. There's more to the story than you've told me, Paul."

"Oh! There you are! For goodness sake!" Mrs. Hadley appeared with their two traveling companions. "Herbert, it's just like you to disappear and be mysterious on a special day like this."

"Well, you know me, Madam. Just call me, Mr. Mysterious." Then the Governor turned to Paul. "I want to discuss this other mystery in more detail when we return. Let's say Friday afternoon at about 4:00. Be sure to have your friend Tobias here as well."

He helped his wife into the carriage and then stepped up into the driver's seat himself. Mrs. Hadley turned to her friends in the back seat, "Did you just hear that conversation? I do swear Herbert can be so mysterious. I never know what to expect next!"

Governor Hadley snapped the reigns and the horses stepped forward down the driveway and out of site.

Mrs. Hadley's words echoed in Paul's mind. "I never know what to expect next. And that has me worried," Paul said to himself.

The Test

At exactly 4:10 on Friday, April 21, 1911 Governor Hadley stepped out of the back door of the Mansion and strode across the lawn to where Paul and Tobias waited. He had been watching them for more than ten minutes from the house. He thought ten minutes was just about enough time for them to get good and nervous. He was right.

Mrs. Hadley had been right also. Her husband did enjoy a good mystery and he also enjoyed watching how people react in various situations. But this was something different. His trusted friend and employee had not been completely honest with him about something happening at his very own home.

Life had seemed to be out of control with all of the things that political parties do, and all of the things people say in newspapers, and all of the things that the citizens want from you. And now, on top of everything else, there was the Capitol fire and all of the planning which had to be done for a new building. And then to find that even his friendship with Paul might not be as good as he had thought. The Governor was feeling irritated, puzzled, and even betrayed as he walked across the lawn that afternoon.

Paul and Tobias had already arranged three sturdy chairs under a pin oak tree near the barn. Tobias made sure to wear his newest overalls and the blue shirt as well as his good shoes. After the Governor sat down, they did also. "Tobias," the Governor said, "tell me about yourself."

Tobias was surprised and shocked that the Governor asked him instead of Paul. "Well, sir, I'm almost fourteen years old..." Then he thought he had better be completely truthful. He started again. "I'm twelve years old and I like horses and..."

The Governor interrupted and said. "Tell me what I don't know. Who are your people? Where is your family from?"

Tobias paused for a second and then began. "I only know as far back as my grandparents. My grandmother was on a farm along with her big sister, Cathay, somewhere close to Jefferson City. My grandfather was a slave too when he was a boy but it wasn't at the same farm. When the war came, they were taken by the blue army to be something called 'collateral' and they had to travel with the army and cook for them, and wash their clothes, and take care of their equipment, and things like that. After the war my grandparents came to Jefferson City and my great aunt, Cathay Williams, became famous. She joined the army and pretended to be a man and she called herself William Cathy. She went out west as a Buffalo Soldier. That's how she got famous."

Governor Hadley looked over at Paul and asked, "Did you know this?"

Paul shook his head to indicate "No."

"Go ahead, son, this is very interesting."

"Well my grandparents worked for people here in the city and they joined the Quinn Chapel. That's the A.M.E. Church. That's where my mother went to church and where I still go to church."

Paul interrupted to tell the Governor, "They have some great cooks there who make sure Tobias gets plenty of vegetables and apple pie."

Governor Hadley asked, "Is this the church just down the hill here on Madison Street?"

Paul answered that it was and then he turned to Tobias, "Sorry to interrupt, Tobias, go ahead please."

Tobias said, "My Pap's family came from somewhere near Fulton but I don't know anything about them. I think they died young because my Pap says that he growed himself."

Paul interrupted again and spoke to the Governor, "Tobias's father sometimes becomes very angry and Tobias doesn't feel safe living there."

"That's right," Tobias continued, "I never know when it's going to happen but he just sort of changes and gets all mad and then I know I have to get out. That's how I ended up in the barn that one night. And then I came back later and kept coming back."

Then the Governor spoke, "The way I'm understanding this is that you don't feel safe going to your father's home and you don't have anywhere else to go. Where do you get your food and how do you get clothes to wear?"

Together Paul and Tobias told the remarkable story of how Tobias got one meal a day from school and one a week from the church. About how he was working now in peoples' gardens in exchange for food and how he had worked for money when the Capitol Building burned. Tobias told about the stale bread from the bakery and about his two sets of clothing. They both told about Tobias's dream to go west like his great aunt Cathay.

Governor Hadley sat for a moment and just thought about what he had heard. Once he looked Tobias right in the eye but Tobias wasn't afraid. He didn't feel that the Governor was the kind of man who would hurt him in any way. If he was a friend of Paul's, he must be a good person also.

Finally the Governor spoke. "Well, I've heard enough for now. But there's more to this story. Tobias, the weather is warm so, unless someone complains, you may continue to use the barn. All I ask is that you respect the property. It's not mine – it belongs to the people. From now on, I want you to come to the west door there each morning and the kitchen staff will have something for your breakfast. I can't imagine going through the day every day on beans and a jelly sandwich."

"Then there's one more thing. If you stay on here, will you be willing to earn your keep by running some errands for me when I need the help?"

"Yes, sir! I sure will! Thank you, sir."

"All right then, that settles it – for now. Tobias, tomorrow is Saturday. I want you to come to the house at 8:00 in the morning for breakfast and then you can run some errands."

He didn't wait for an answer. The Governor was used to giving orders and this time he wasn't asking anything. This time it was business. This time it was an order. This time instead of being a little boy hiding in the dark, Tobias was being treated like a man.

Saturday Morning

Late April is usually a beautiful time in Missouri. The spring rains and southerly breezes have turned everything green and even the cut grass has a special smell from the little onions that grow in it. This morning was one of the best. It was warm and sunny with little puffy clouds in the sky when Tobias knocked politely on the west door of the Mansion.

He was a little nervous as the kitchen staff kept looking at him. Then he realized that he was something of a mystery to them. He decided that he liked being mysterious. This morning he knew secrets that everyone else in the room wanted to know.

They brought him a plate with scrambled eggs, two strips of bacon, and some tiny little slices of potatoes, fried and good. Then someone brought him a glass of orange juice and a glass of milk and another small plate with buttered toast. He sat and looked at it for a few seconds and then he stated, "This is too much. Do I have to eat it all? I can't eat this much."

A lady with gray hair pulled up into a bun on top of her head stepped forward. "We didn't know what to expect," she said. "We didn't want to make too little so we made too much, I suppose. After this we will bring a small breakfast and you can always feel free to ask for more if you wish. Is that fair?"

Tobias tried to hide his wet eyes. He was thinking, "FAIR? Is that fair? It was going to be wonderful." Without looking directly at the lady he said, "Thank you, ma'am, for your kindness." Then he smiled to himself when he thought about his winter coat. That certainly would not fit him next year.

It only took a few minutes for Tobias to eat his fill and the lady with the gray hair brought him two envelopes. "These are the errands that the Governor wants you to take care of today. Can you read what's on the envelopes?"

"Yes, ma'am, I can read," he answered. Then he saw that the first envelope was for Jensen's Dry Goods Store. He knew where that was. It's where he bought his clothes in February. The second envelope was addressed to the A.M.E. Church. He certainly knew where that was.

Tobias asked if he could leave now and the ladies all smiled and "shooshed" him out the door. As he walked toward the store he noticed that the envelopes weren't sealed. He shouldn't – but he did – he peeked inside. The one to the store was just some sort of note to someone there. The one to the church was fat. He looked inside and his heart stopped. It was full of five dollar bills. There must have been at least a hundred dollars in there!

He didn't like having that much money with him. There were too many people who would happily kill a boy if they knew he had that much money. He stuffed the money envelope down into the big front pocket of his overalls and hoped that no one could tell anything was there. He also decided to go the long way around to the church. There was one saloon where his father's friends liked to hang out and Tobias didn't want to get anywhere near them on this morning.

At Jensen's store Tobias walked up to the young man at the counter and told him, "I'm Tobias and I…"

"We've been waiting for you, Tobias," the man said. "Here's your package."

Tobias thanked the man and said, "I'll get it right to Governor Hadley."

The man laughed and said, "Oh, I don't think the Governor wants these things. The package has your name on it."

Outside the store and just around the corner, Tobias peeked inside the stiff brown paper and found two new shirts, some new overalls and some other things he couldn't make out. "I guess he wants me to look right if I'm going to be doing errands for him," he thought. Tobias was especially happy because he was ashamed to be seen in his old clothes that he had worn the night of the fire. They didn't even fit him any more and people could see his legs between the bottom of the pants and the top of his shoes. He was way too old to be dressed like that!

When he got to the church, Brother Curry took the envelope and opened it. Then he looked long and full at Tobias. "Son, where did you get this money?"

"A gray haired lady with her hair pulled up gave it to me this morning," he said. Seeing that Brother Curry didn't understand, Tobias said, "She works at the Governor's Mansion and this is something Governor Hadley wanted me to bring to you."

Brother Curry was overwhelmed by the sight of a boy pulling a plain envelope out of his pants pocket and then handing over a stack of money. He was even more overwhelmed by the story that some gray-haired lady and the Governor had sent it. If the truth were told, Brother Curry probably didn't believe that Tobias had been at the Governor's Mansion or that he had anything to do with the lady or the Governor.

Then he took the money out of the envelope and found a small note tucked inside. It was signed H.S. Hadley and it said, "I hope this helps with the good work you do in your church kitchen."

Brother Curry sat down and looked at the stack of five dollar bills and then looked up at Tobias. He smiled a huge smile and said, "Child, you have some explaining to do!"

****

On Tuesday, Tobias, wearing a new shirt, went to the barn after school and Paul was already there. Soon Governor Hadley appeared with a letter in his hand. "Tobias I got a letter from Reverend Curry. He certainly thinks a lot of you and he remembers your mother and grandparents fondly. I want to know – What did you think when you saw the money in that envelope?"

Paul looked with surprise at both of them. He had known nothing about Saturday's errands.

Tobias answered the Governor, "I was scared when I saw the money. I thought I had better not go my usual way to church because there are some bad people at that one tavern and I didn't want to get near them."

"You know, my note didn't say how much money was in there. You could have taken a little of the money and no one would ever know."

"That would be stealing, sir. That would be stealing from you or from my church or – I don't know for sure but I wouldn't do that!"

The Governor just nodded his head, turned and walked away toward the house.

"I don't understand!" Tobias said. Did I do something wrong?"

"No," Paul answered, "You did something very right. And you just made a friend for life. A very powerful and important friend for life."

History

As the Spring turned into Summer, a curious thing happened. Governor Hadley began to spend more of the warm evenings behind the House. His wife, Agnes, still preferred to sit under the trees in the front yard or maybe in the house. But, in the yard, she could be seen and see everybody who wanted to stop and say hello. The Governor tired of meeting people he hardly knew and preferred the company of Paul and Tobias.

When Paul went home to his wife at the end of each day, it would sometimes leave just Governor Hadley and his young admirer. One breezy evening Tobias dared to ask the Governor a very serious question. "Sir, do you think a black man might ever be the Governor?"

The Governor collected his thoughts and replied. "You know, Tobias, politics is all about numbers. Will there ever be enough black men and women to elect a Governor? I doubt it. Will there ever be enough Osage Indians? Probably not. But will there ever be enough women? I'll bet that will come pretty soon. You see, the women are already voting in many places and there are so many of them that it's just a matter of time until they get together and elect a woman."

"Black men are voting but there just aren't very many of them in the state. About the only way that we will see a black man or woman as Governor is if we can forget about all of the awful things that people come up with about the races. I think that will take a few generations. Maybe your great-grandchildren would have the chance."

"Here's something to think about. In your Bible stories at church, do you ever read about those people voting?"

"No, sir," Tobias answered.

"That's right nobody got to vote back then. It has taken us thousands of years to get to this point but now things are moving pretty fast. It used to be that only men with property could vote. Then it was all white men. Then it was all the white men and black men and now it's the women too in most places. It's all happening pretty fast and that's good. Pretty exciting, don't you think?"

"Yes, sir. To hear you tell it, it's almost like I'm watching history."

"Tobias, son, you are watching history. You've seen the automobile come and electric lights. In another five years all of the stage coaches will be gone from Missouri – replaced by motor buses. Bridges are replacing ferry boats. You will be able to tell your children that you remember the old Capitol Building and watched them build the new one. You're seeing history being made every day."

After that day, Tobias always looked at things in a different way. He realized that things were always changing and that the world he knew would be very different from the world that his children would know. He was living Missouri's history and America's history just by living his own life. It made him feel like he really was a part of it all.

Baseball

It was Monday, May 29 and school was out for the summer. Tobias knew exactly what he wanted to do on this day. Jackson, a friend at church, had told him of a new professional baseball team that had started. They were called the Jefferson City Senators and today they were scheduled to play the Kirksville Osteopaths. His friend had promised to show him how to get into the baseball game for free.

When he got to the ballpark his friend was waiting along with three other boys. One of the others was an older boy from his school and the other two boys were white and Tobias didn't know them. Tobias walked over to meet Jackson and the other boys nodded their heads as he approached. The white boys were older and they were wearing gloves. Tobias wondered if they might be on the team.

"Hi, Jackson," Tobias said. "How can we get into the game for free?"

Jackson explained that they would "shag flies" during batting practice. He said that when the power hitters would hit a ball out of the park Tobias should run and get it. "When we both have a ball," Jackson explained, "we take them up to the ticket window and give it to them. Then they let us in to sit in the bleachers. That way they don't have to buy so many baseballs and we get to see the game."

Just then a ball came flying over the wall and landed in some tall grass near one of the boys with a glove. He scooped it up and held the prize high for everyone to see. The other boys congratulated him and turned quickly to watch for the next fly ball. Soon one sailed over the fence and bounced once in front of Tobias who grabbed it before it could get by. Jackson slapped him on the back and the other boys yelled things like, "Good one," and "Nice grab."

Then a ball came sailing high in the air and completely over the heads of the boys. They all ran to retrieve it but Tobias got there first. Now there were two free passes available for Tobias and Jackson and it was time to turn them in at the ticket window. Soon they found a shady spot in the right field bleachers and got to watch the rest of the batting and fielding practice. In time all of the boys from outside were sitting with them in the right field bleachers.

Tobias had never seen professional baseball players and he marveled at how good they were. He had played baseball at school but these men could hit the ball so high that it seemed to go out of sight. Then an outfielder seemed to be waiting for it when it finally came down. He loved the uniforms and the little Dixieland band that played their way through the stadium. He loved being a part of something this big. He loved it that all these people were there together having fun. Just about the only thing he didn't love was that the Kirksville Osteopaths beat the Jefferson City Senators that day.

As they left, Jackson showed Tobias the team schedule and they saw that on Wednesday, Hannibal's Cannibals would be in town and the boys planned to meet again for another day of fun at the old ball park. When Tobias got back to the Mansion barn he was amazed that Paul didn't know much about the Senators. "I used to go to a Kansas City Blues game from time to time," he said. "That was before I moved here of course. Maybe I'll try to see a game if they ever play when I'm not working."

Tobias daydreamed about baseball for the rest of the day and promised himself that he would see many more games that summer. He could not have known that he wouldn't be able to see many games at all. He could not have guessed the wonderful reason why he would see so few games.

Appaloosa

One of those soft summer evenings when Paul hadn't yet left for home, the three friends sat talking in the shadow of the barn. The Governor asked, "Well, Tobias, how are your preparations coming for your ranching career?"

The Governor always talked that way and Tobias was getting used to it but he wasn't sure just what the man meant.

"I mean, are you saving money? – Are you getting better at riding and roping? – Can you play a harmonica or a guitar?"

"I don't know anything about music," Tobias answered, "but I am saving money. And for riding, well, I never have been on a horse."

The Governor looked at Paul. Paul shrugged his shoulders and said, "We don't have any riding horses. He's never been anywhere where people ride. He's a city boy."

"Well he's not staying a city boy," the Governor insisted. "Who ever heard of a ranch hand who can't ride a horse? We have to do something about this."

"Do something about what?" It was Mrs. Hadley coming across the lawn.

"Agnes, we have an aspiring rancher who can't ride a horse! We must get him some time in the saddle!"

"Oh joy!" She said. "Tomorrow is Saturday and we can visit the Ledbetters and while we visit, Tobias can ride. I'm sure they'll loan him one of their gentle horses if we all say please."

Everyone looked at Tobias and the Governor boomed out, "Well, what say you, Tobias? Will we meet some horses tomorrow?"

Tobias just answered with his big smile. A smile that he used more and more these days.

****

The next morning Tobias hitched up the carriage (by himself for the first time). Mrs. Hadley had asked if they could take a carriage instead of the automobile. The Governor didn't even check Tobias's work. He just trusted Tobias to do it right. They all climbed into the carriage and went down to the landing. There Tobias climbed out and led the horses onto the ferry boat. He stayed with them and kept them calm while the little steamboat made its way across the strong current. Mr. and Mrs. Hadley greeted their fellow passengers.

As they made the slow trip across the mighty river Tobias looked up at the giant bridge that spanned the river high above them. There were a few automobiles crossing in both directions and Tobias marveled at how small they looked way up there. He had never ridden in an automobile – maybe someday he would. For now he was happy to see the bridge from this new perspective.

On the north bank, Tobias led the horses and the carriage off the ferry and held the team while Mr. and Mrs. Hadley got back in. Then he jumped into the back seat and they were off. As they rode Tobias waited for a chance to speak and when the adults grew quiet he asked, "Why didn't we cross on the bridge? Why doesn't everyone just go across the bridge?"

Governor Hadley answered that horses are often frightened by bridges. "That's why they build covered bridges," he said. "It would be a disaster if a horse or a team of horses was running wild on the bridge. And can you imagine trying to drive a herd of cattle or hogs across the bridge? So the Steam Ferry takes people with farm animals and farm products across. Maybe someday those things can travel by trucks or trains but I hope that we will always have a place for ferry boats on our rivers."

Within about fifteen minutes the Governor turned onto a smaller road and approached a beautiful white house with several white barns and corn cribs behind it. Then Ledbetters seemed pleasantly surprised to see the Hadleys. They sat on the front porch while one of their daughters went for lemonade. When they learned of Tobias and his wish to ride a horse, the oldest Ledbetter boy offered to help Tobias. On the way to the horse barn the boy said, "Thank you. I thought I was going to have to sit still with my mouth shut for who knows how long!"

"My name is Patrick," the boy said. "Is this your first time to ride, Tobias?"

Patrick found a horse that he promised to be a gentle one but it was very tall. Tobias was intimidated by its size. "What kind of horse is this?" Tobias asked.

53

"Well, you see she's gray and she has all these black and white spots on her hind quarter. That means she's an appaloosa. That's a kind of Indian horse – from the Nez Perce tribe I think. This is a great cow pony. They're very popular out west."

When the horse was saddled and bridled, Patrick helped Tobias to get settled on her. "Always approach from the left," he said. "Left foot in the stirrup and swing your right leg over. That's it. Now just sit tall and gently pull the reigns left or right when you want to turn."

Patrick stepped back and said, "Go ahead now and take her around the corral a few times and then I'll open the gate and you can do some real riding."

Soon Patrick was back in the shade of the front porch and everyone could see Tobias stopping, starting, turning this way and that. Sometimes he walked the horse and sometimes he trotted her. All the while he sat tall and erect.

"That guy's a natural," Patrick observed.

"He's good with horses," the Governor put in. "He just never had an opportunity to ride one."

The group tried several times to get Tobias's attention but, if he saw them, he didn't act like it. Finally he rode back to the house and stopped in front of the porch to collect compliments. Patrick reminded him, "Just stand in the left stirrup and swing your leg over to get down."

When Tobias's right foot hit the ground, the rest of him didn't stop. His entire body crashed in a heap on the grass next to the horse. She just looked around at him and then looked away. Tobias tried to stand up but couldn't. His legs wouldn't work any more.

"That's why we were trying to get you to come back earlier,"

Mr. Ledbetter said. "Riding isn't so hard but you really have to get used to a saddle. Those things take your legs away."

While the Hadleys were getting into the carriage and saying their goodbyes, Tobias walked around and checked the team and the hitch. He thanked Patrick for his help and then climbed into the back seat.

On the way to the ferry, Mrs. Hadley asked, "Well, Tobias, do you still have an interest in being a western rancher?"

"Oh, yes, ma'am," he said. "And will the country out west be as pretty as this?"

"The west will have things like mountains that we don't have much of here," the Governor answered. "But you won't see much of this beautiful green. Most of the west is dry and brown."

Tobias had never thought of a place not being green. That boggled his mind a little. But, more than that, his mind was full of the joy of floating across the countryside on the back of a gentle, powerful, beautiful animal. Today had been one of the best days of his life.

He would ride many hundreds of horses in his life but he would always have a love for the Appaloosa breed. And he would always recall that day when a city boy was by himself in wide green fields atop a tall gray horse.

August 2

The previous day, August 1, Missouri's voters had approved a statewide referendum to raise money for building a bigger and better new Capitol in Jefferson City. It was the talk of everyone in Jefferson City. It meant that the city would continue to be the center of Missouri's government. Some people had wanted to move it back to St. Louis.

When Tobias went to breakfast on the morning of August 2 there was a strange commotion going on in the house. There was a constant knocking on the front door and people were cutting across the lawn rather that walking around the proper way on the street. Everyone on the staff seemed upset and Tobias could hear Mrs. Hadley speaking in a louder-than-usual voice and telling people that the Governor was in his temporary office on Capitol Drive.

Tobias thanked the ladies and left as soon as he could. As he walked back toward the barn, he looked down the hill and saw that the streets were choked with people. Huge numbers of people were coming up from the train station and the ferry boat. He made a quick decision to put on his best clothes and go into the streets to see what all the excitement was about.

Even though it was early morning the place was already terribly crowded because over 1600 people were there to see the lawmakers and the Governor. Of course the Capitol Building was gone and the streets around it were cluttered with construction equipment so this made things even worse. The Senators and Representatives had offices all around the town but people were having trouble finding them. The Legislature had been meeting in the Cole County Courthouse but had now moved to the Library at St. Peter's School. The Senate had just moved over to the Supreme Courts Building. It was a terrible mess.

To make matters worse, the crowds and all of the things they brought were blocking the streets and the Jefferson and High Street Trolley couldn't make its rounds. As it tried to make its journey down High Street in front of the capitol ruins, people kept stepping in front of it. The conductor was not only making all the noise he could with his bell, but he was even yelling at the people in the streets. Some of them began to yell back at the conductor. The passengers either joined in the yelling or gave up and got off to walk to their destinations.

Tobias soon learned that a new highway was to be built from the east coast all the way to the Pacific. These people all wanted the new highway to come through their town. The big decision was whether it should go from St. Louis on the south side of the river through Jefferson City and Sedalia to Kansas City – or should it go from St. Louis on the north side of the river through St. Charles, Columbia and Boonville to Kansas City. And, of course which smaller towns would be included or by-passed.

Everyone was giving away mementos of their towns and encouraging people to remember them. Others were busy trying to make deals with neighboring towns and cities. Some were setting up to cook food and give it away! Tobias went from booth to booth seeing what free items were to be found.

He discovered that the free things weren't really for him. They were for the "important" people who could make the decisions or could give advice to the decision-makers. He also discovered that people could recognize that he wasn't really important because he was the only one there wearing overalls. Overalls may be great for when you're working but these men all wore pants with braces.

One stand was making and giving away donuts and Tobias asked if he might have one. He had never tasted one and it looked so good! It smelled even better!

"Go away, son," the man in the booth said. "These are for important people. Are you an important person?" Then he put his head back and laughed. Everyone nearby laughed with him.

Tobias, as always, remained polite. "No, sir. I'm no one important. I just take care of Governor Hadley's horses and carriages. I'm his errand boy."

The crowd grew quiet for just a second and then everyone started writing notes and invitations. They crammed them into Tobias's pockets along with gifts and souvenirs of all sorts. He left for a minute and then came right back with two large feed bags folded over his arm.

"Hey look!" someone said. "It's the Governor's errand boy! He takes messages to the Governor." Soon both bags were filled with gifts for Tobias and notes for the Governor.

By the end of the day Tobias had made three trips to the streets below the Mansion. He had eaten food that he never dreamed of and he even met a man giving away bratwurst. "Good mit mustard!" Tobias said.

"Ya, Ya," the man replied and he gave Tobias a generous helping of the spicy German mustard. "You tell Governor, good food in Hermann. Good friends in Hermann."

"Yes, sir, I will," Tobias promised and he chomped down on the sausage to emphasize his point.

That night Tobias had terrible nightmares because of all the rich food and sweet treats. He still felt a little wobbly the next morning when he walked into the Governor's office with hundreds of hand-written notes and advertisements.

Governor Hadley looked up from his desk and shook his head. All he could say was, "Oh, Tobias!"

Trousers

The summer was such a good time! Tobias continued to work for people in their gardens but now he didn't just get paid in food that he could eat raw. Instead he brought most of the food back to the kitchen staff and they would do wonderful things with it. Tobias was proud that food he was growing was feeding some of the finest people in the state. He also felt as if he was paying his own way more than he could have done in the past.

He continued to be a trusted errand boy for Governor Hadley and he continued to help Paul with the horses and the work around the barn. As August wore on, he looked forward to seeing his friends again at school but he knew that he would miss the opportunities of this summer with Paul and Governor and Mrs. Hadley.

One hot summer morning Tobias visited all of the people who used him to help in their gardens. "It's just too hot today," they would say. Or, "The garden's in good shape. Let's rest for a day or two." Not a single person needed Tobias to help them on this steamy day.

He went back to the barn thinking of a shady spot and some cool water. He was happy to see that Paul was in the stables today because Tobias had questions. "Paul," he began, "did you see all of the people who were here about the roads? They were from all over the state."

"I saw them," Paul replied, "and I tried to avoid them. What a mob!"

"Well I went down there and looked around a lot. And, Paul, I was the only guy there wearing overalls. Those men were from all over and not one of them had overalls. In fact, they wouldn't give me donuts or anything because I was wearing overalls."

"I never thought about that." Paul said. "But I'll bet that most of those men wear bib overalls at home when they're working in their gardens or on their farms. When they get dressed up for special things they put on trousers with braces."

"Do you have trousers and braces?" Tobias wanted to know.

"Yes, I do. But I wear overalls when I'm working. I usually just wear trousers to church or on the train."

"Do people out west wear overalls or trousers?"

"Some wear overalls but most of them that ride horses wear trousers. They have a special kind of trousers made out of canvas. Usually blue canvas. They're very tough pants but they still wear a leather covering over the pants called chaps."

Tobias was fascinated. "Can I get some blue canvas pants with braces?"

"Now, that's another thing," Paul said. "I believe that most of those western guys don't wear braces at all. They wear belts around their middles. The pants have special loops on them to hold the belts. Strange, don't you think?"

Paul continued. "I'll tell you what, Tobias. They know you over at Jensen's Store. Go over there some day and ask them to see some blue 'Levi' pants. Levi Strauss is the guy who invented the things. You try on a pair and, if you like them, you can use some of your money to buy a pair."

Tobias hadn't thought about actually getting any new pants. He was mostly just curious. He certainly never considered digging out that tin container and taking any money out. But then he thought about just trying them on. That wouldn't cost anything.

By afternoon Tobias was finished with thinking. He walked over to Jensen's. The same young man was behind the counter today and he greeted Tobias as he entered. He helped Tobias to try some pants that were a lot like overalls with no bib. But these things were tighter and stiffer. They weren't nearly so comfortable. They felt funny. When he looked in a mirror, he also thought they looked funny.

"Is this the way they're supposed to fit?" Tobias asked.

"Not exactly," the young clerk answered. "These are a little too tight and when you wash them, they'll shrink so they'll be even tighter. You know, most men buy them larger and let them shrink. If you get them a little too long, you just roll a cuff on the bottom. Men who ride horses wear those boots with tall heels so they need the pants to be a little longer. You just buy them to fit the way you want.

Tobias tried on another pair – this time two sizes larger. They felt better and looked like they would last longer if he grew any taller. Tobias also noticed that they made him look taller and thinner than he usually looked in his bib overalls.

"They're two dollars and two bits. Can I wrap them up for you?" the clerk asked.

Tobias replied that $2.25 was a lot of money. He would need to think this over. And he did think it over all the way home. The minute he got to the barn he dug out his tin container and took out three dollars. That should be enough to pay for the new jeans and a good leather belt to keep them up.

The next morning Tobias put on his favorite shirt and his new jeans and went to breakfast. Everyone there told him that somehow he looked taller and older today. He couldn't even remember what he ate. He was too busy soaking in compliments and feeling good about himself and the new jeans he had worked for and saved for.

Immediately after breakfast he went back to the barn and changed into his regular clothes and carefully folded his favorites so they would be nice for church on Sunday. He wondered what Esther would think.

****

Tobias was using some of the polish that he used on harnesses but this time he was polishing his shoes. He was just finishing when someone called his name. He looked out to see one of the yard men waving to him. "Tobias," he yelled, "The Governor is calling for you."

When he arrived at the Governor's temporary office he was surprised to see Mrs. Hadley there also. Governor Hadley was just saying goodbye to a man who was carrying a white straw hat. He motioned for Tobias to have a seat. Mrs. Hadley smiled and asked if he had been getting any work.

Tobias explained to her about the gardens and the heat and the dry weather. "All in all," he said, "people just aren't doing much in their gardens right now."

Governor Hadley closed the door and said, "That's exactly why I wanted to see you today. I was speaking with Mr. Ledbetter this morning – you remember the Ledbetters, don't you? – of course you do. Well, I was speaking with Mr. Ledbetter and he said things are changing on the farm. For one thing, folks are driving around in automobiles and they aren't riding horses as much. That makes the price of horses drop way down."

"He also said that so many young men are going off to college or off to work in the city that he can't find people to help him on the farm. He's offered a good job for just a while if you would like to help him out."

"You have over a month before school starts again and he said that, if you will help him to put up hay and do other jobs for thirty days, he will let you live in his bunkhouse and he will provide meals and pay you $2.25 a day. He'll also make sure that you get a horse to ride back home so you can go to church on Sundays. By the time school starts, you'll have over $45.00. He is also offering to sell you that Appaloosa horse and a fair quality saddle for $45.00 if you choose. You could keep the horse in our barn here at the Mansion. Or you could just keep the $45.00 if you choose to do that."

Tobias just couldn't stay seated. He stood beside his chair and then walked around behind it and toward the door as he said, "I don't know how to put up hay but I can learn. If I go by and pick up my clothes, do you think I can walk all the way to Ledbetters by dark?"

Mrs. Hadley put her hands together and held them in front of her face to hide her laughter. Governor Hadley yelled, "Whoa back there, cowpoke! I know there's a mustang inside there but reign him in a little. You do what you need to do today and tomorrow after breakfast I'm certain that Paul will be happy to run you out to the Ledbetters in the small carriage."

Haying

On Tobias's first day with the Ledbetters they were beginning the haying. Patrick walked behind a team of spotted draft horses as they pulled a big machine with moving blades sticking way out on the side. As the wheels of the machine turned, they made the blades slide back and forth and big waves of tall grass fell behind the machine.

Patrick held the reigns to "steer" the horses but mostly he talked to them to tell them what to do. He only needed four words to tell them every thing they needed to know. "Giddap" meant to go forward. "Gee" meant to turn right. "Haw" meant to turn left and "Whoa" meant to stop. At first Tobias just walked along with Patrick while Patrick explained a million little things about the job he was doing. Then he gave the reigns to Tobias and Patrick walked with him. In no time Tobias was cutting hay like a professional. He didn't know that the horses knew exactly what to do and he was really just following while they did their jobs.

They mowed even more the next day and then they began to rake the cut grass. To rake the hay, the team of draft horses pulled a large rake with spinning fingers of steel that picked up the cut hay, turned it over and laid it in long straight rows across the field. Finally they brought out a hay wagon. They loaded as much as they could onto the wagon by throwing it up with long pitch forks.

The sun was beating down and the men were all sweating. Small pieces of straw and chaff flew through the air and stuck to the sweaty bodies of the workers. The itching was terrible. Patrick yelled, "Hey,

Tobias. Just concentrate on how good it's going to feel to get under the pump this evening."

Once all the hay was taken back to the homestead, it was a several-day process to feed it into a big steam-powered baler and compactor. It was another hot and itchy job but not nearly as bad as the days of pitching the hay. On Saturday afternoon everyone was told to go on home early with full pay. Tobias was probably happier than anyone there to hear the good news.

After his turn under the water pump Patrick led him to the barn. "You can pick any horse you want to ride home today except those three. They're some special horses and my dad's really particular about them."

"Can I take the Appaloosa mare?" Tobias wanted to know.

"Sure. But you've already ridden her. You might want to ride some different horses and see which one you like best." Tobias didn't say it but he was working in order to buy that particular mare. She was an Appaloosa. She was an Indian horse. She was a great cow pony. She was going to be Tobias's horse.

When Tobias climbed up on that big mare this time he wasn't limited by any fences. He rode right on down the drive and turned left on the main road to the ferry. Whether the entire world was actually watching or not, he felt as if it was and he rode tall in the saddle and held the reigns just above the saddle horn. He had seen a million pictures. He knew exactly how he wanted to do this.

When he got off the ferry on the south bank he noticed an old black couple selling hats woven of straw. Some were broad-brimmed and looked like they would protect him from the sun. They looked too much like farmer's hats and not quite enough like cowboy's hats but they only cost ten cents. "Will you be here on Monday?" he asked the couple.

"We'll be here Monday morning," they said. "But by Monday afternoon we'll be at Rocheport."

"I just paid the ferryman my only dime," Tobias said. I'll see you on Monday."

"Come here, Boy," the old man said. "Ride that fine animal over here. Now you take this big-brimmer and pay us for it on Monday. A man riding a fine horse into town needs a fine hat on his head."

Tobias tried on the hat and it was a perfect fit. "Wow! Fits perfect!" he said.

The old man smiled. "You know horses – I know hats."

"I surely thank you, sir. I'll see you early on Monday morning."

Tobias rode one more block up the hill but chose not to turn the Appaloosa in to the barn. Instead, he rode around the block so he could come past the front of the Governor's Mansion. He saw Governor Hadley reach to touch Mrs. Hadley's elbow and she put one hand up to her mouth. Then everyone on the front lawn waved to him. All of the important people waved to Tobias – a tall man on horseback with a broad-brimmed hat!

Heaven

At church on Sunday morning the sermon was about Heaven and the pleasures that await us there. Brother Curry really knew how to keep a person's attention and Tobias was no exception. But he was so busy thinking about the minister's message that he wasn't prepared when Brother Curry said, "I'm sure we all have some ideas of Heaven. Ideas of the best of the best. Ideas of things more wonderful than our favorite things on earth."

Then he did it. He pointed right at Tobias and said, "Tobias what things might a person see on the streets of Heaven?"

Tobias couldn't think of what to say so he blurted out, "Bratwurst mit mustard and donuts."

There was pure silence in the room as every head turned and looked at Tobias. He wanted to shrink down into the pew but that wasn't his way so he just sat right up and looked Brother Curry in the eye.

"Tobias, son, I don't think I understand what you just said."

"You asked about wonderful things we've experienced here on earth and I thought of bratwurst mit mustard and then donuts."

"OK, I understand now about the donuts but what else was that?"

Tobias explained to everyone about the man from the German restaurant and about the other man from Hermann and about those good sausages and mustard. All around the church heads began to bob as people understood. Brother Curry said, "I know at least one person is getting my message this morning. Earthly delights can be wonderful but where can things be even more wonderful?"

Tobias answered, "In Heaven!'

"Hallelujah and Amen" echoed all through Quinn Chapel.

****

After Sunday Service everyone went to the church basement to talk while the ladies of the congregation warmed the food and set it out for the noon meal. Of course Tobias was wearing his new blue jeans and one of the shirts the Governor had given to him. It was a bright plaid and, when tucked into the jeans you could see his new belt. Of course his shoes were as black and shiny as one of the Governor's harnesses. Being indoors, his broad-brimmed hat was tucked under his arm.

Tobias was surprised at the reaction his clothes got from the "church family." Paul and the Hadleys had remarked about him looking prosperous, or taller, or older. They had given him smiling compliments. None of the folks at church were smiling as they looked at him.

The lady who made the wonderful apple pies came across the room and asked, "Are things going well for you now, Tobias?"

"Yes, ma'am," he answered, "Very well!"

"Tobias, you know that we love you and care about you."

"Yes, ma'am?"

"Well, I'm just going to speak my piece," she said. "Today you look like a young man – a wealthy young man. I hope you haven't done something you shouldn't to come by these fine clothes or the fine horse one of the sisters saw you riding on Saturday."

"Ma'am, I certainly have done something. I have been working to clean up after the big fire and now I work at a farm across the river. It's only for a few weeks until school starts again but it's a good job. They're good people and they pay me very well and let me use the horse. I hope to buy that horse one day."

"Oh, Tobias," she said, "I knew we could be proud of you. As she hugged him, several of the men slapped him on the back and said things like, "Good for you, son," and "Blessings on you, Tobias."

When the time came to pass through the line for food, Tobias filled his plate with a chicken leg, vegetables, greens, and cornbread. Of course he saved room for apple pie if there happened to be some today. It was so hot, however, that he knew most of the women would not be baking.

To his surprise, a family came to sit in the empty seats across the table from him. That in itself wasn't surprising but this family consisted of the shy Esther and her parents and little sister. They mentioned his western-style clothes but Esther said almost nothing. That was OK Tobias thought. He understood that she was very quiet. That was one of the things that made her special.

The Orphan Train

It was a beautiful Sunday afternoon and Tobias had a few hours with nothing planned. Then he remembered seeing a notice that made him curious. Tacked onto a tree, the sign said that an orphan train would be arriving and that everyone was invited to come and make selections. Tobias had been living there just one block from the train station and he had seen all sorts of trains but he couldn't figure out just what an orphan train might be.

So at 3:00 sharp that afternoon the train from the east pulled in to the station and Tobias was there to watch. To his surprise, several children got off and then many more. Soon there were over a hundred young children and a few not-so-young being herded into lines on the railroad platform. Mayor Heinrichs and some of the leading citizens of Jefferson City were there to see that everything went well.

When the children were all lined up, the local people began to walk through the lines and ask the children questions. A few men even reached out and felt the muscles in the boys' arms. Soon the local adults began to say things like, "I'll take this one." or "I can use both of these." The children helplessly followed the adults who signed for them and then got into wagons, carriages, or automobiles and drove away.

Tobias heard one old grandmother talking to a girl who was about his age. "I'm getting old and maybe I'm not much fun any more," she said, "but my only daughter died of diphtheria when she was just about your age. If you will come and live with me, I promise to always treat you well and we can make a new family. What do you say?"

The girl smiled and nodded her head and the new little family went to the recorder's table.

One farm couple said, "We'll take these two boys," and tugged their arms so they would follow. But the boys planted their feet and stood still. They were in a group of siblings with themselves and a younger brother and a very small sister. The adults took the boys by the wrists and began pulling the boys away and the little girl screamed while her youngest brother cried.

"Here, here!" the mayor yelled. "There's no need for that. Why not take all four? Or take two others."

"These are the ones I want," the farmer said. There aren't two others up here as strong as those two."

The mayor's face was getting red, "Are you looking for children or for beasts of burden? If you want a mule or an ox, this is not the place! I think you should leave now!"

One girl stood very quietly on the left side of the group. Tobias thought she looked frightened. Her eyes were very sad and very wet. Her quiet nature and the way she stood reminded Tobias of Esther.

Then the engineer blew the train's whistle and the children hurried back onto the train and toward the next stop. As quickly as the spectacle had begun, it was over.

****

Tobias was puzzled and very troubled by what he had just witnessed. He walked over to Brother Curry's home next to the church. Luckily Brother Curry was there. Tobias explained what he had just seen and asked his pastor, "Is this some kind of slavery? These children were white and I thought slavery was over anyway."

Brother Curry said that the Orphan Trains had been running for almost fifty years now and that it wasn't slavery but it could be very sad. The children had no good homes in the big cities of the east so they were put on trains and sent to the Midwest where it was hoped that some nice families would adopt them.

"It might seem terrible to watch, Tobias, but the fact is that over 100,000 children now have homes when they didn't before. And most of the children have been very well-treated and are happy. Those who might not be well-treated are removed and placed in a better home. It's turning out to be a pretty good thing."

Brother Curry was a thoughtful and considerate person and he didn't mention the fact that Tobias was himself a homeless child. But Tobias understood more than most of us just what it felt like to be alone, lonely, vulnerable, and scared.

The Adventure

It was Monday and the sun was just lighting the eastern sky when Tobias climbed into the saddle and nudged the Appaloosa down the hill to Jefferson Landing to meet the ferry. The old couple with the hats had not arrived so Tobias was arranging to leave ten cents with the ferryman for the couple when he saw them coming. He rode his horse down the riverbank to meet them and gave them the money he owed and thanked them again.

Tobias trotted the horse back up the riverbank and got to the ferry just in time for it to push off. This time he talked with people on the ferry boat just as the Governor had done earlier. People were very nice to him. Was it the possession of a horse that made the difference or had his attitude changed and people could see that? Or was it that he was outgrowing his shyness as he matured? The answer probably isn't important. What matters is that Tobias was a good and likeable person and the world was a friendlier place than he might have realized.

The farm work was hard and it was also exhilarating. Tobias could see that his shirts fit him differently as his shoulders grew. He loved the open space of the great river valley. He learned to appreciate the passing of a cloud which gave him temporary relief from the sun. He loved the summer showers that swept through and left him cool and his clothing wet. As the clothing dried it also cooled and took away the weariness that summer afternoons on the farm can bring.

From time to time Tobias would go to the bunkhouse and look at the chart that he kept showing how much he had earned. He didn't want to leave that much money in a tin container behind some hay bales so he asked Mr. Ledbetter to pay him at the end of the summer.

Tobias learned to look forward to Saturdays and loved the Ledbetter custom of quitting early on Saturdays. The time under the pump on Saturday afternoons cleansed his skin, his clothing, and his spirit. No matter how dirty he may have been, he still felt clean and proud astride his Appaloosa as he headed home.

On one of those trips he started to wonder about taking a different ride. An adventure to someplace more distant. A day to be independent and completely on his own. A day with the Appaloosa.

Tobias told Paul of his idea for an adventure. But Paul reminded him that he didn't own the horse. He needed to wait just a little while longer and then with the title to the horse in his possession, he could go anywhere he wanted.

"Alright," said Tobias, "how about a different kind of adventure? I've always wanted to go on a train. Could I go some day and ride the train?"

"Now, that's completely up to you," Paul answered. "But you do have obligations. You can't let the Ledbetters down or the Governor."

"I could go on a Sunday," Tobias suggested. Nobody wants me to work for them on Sundays."

"Would the people at church worry if you weren't there?"

"Oh, they would," Tobias replied. "But I could tell Brother Curry and he could tell everyone else so they wouldn't worry about me."

"The ticket window is still open at the train station," Paul commented. "You could run down there right now and see where you might like to go and see if you're willing to spend that much of your money for a ticket."

The station was only one block away and downhill all the way. Tobias's feet just barely touched the ground as he flew to the station. At the window he asked the agent where the trains go.

"Where they go?" the man said. "Son, this is 1911. Trains go almost everywhere! You could go west toward California, Sedalia, Kansas City or Independence." Or you could go east toward Hermann or New Haven or . . ."

"Wait a minute! How much does it cost to go to Hermann?"

"Round trip?"

Tobias didn't answer and the ticket agent looked to see his puzzled expression. "I mean do you want to go there and come back?"

"Oh yes, sir. I have to come back because the Governor and the Ledbetters need me."

This time the ticket agent was the one with the puzzled expression but he decided not to ask. "One round trip ticket to Hermann – and back – would be eighty five cents."

Tobias counted out exactly eighty five cents and took his ticket for next Sunday's train. Then he went back home and put the ticket into the tin container behind the back hay bales.

At church the next morning he sought out Brother Curry and told him not to worry next Sunday because he was taking a trip. "A trip!" Rev. Curry exclaimed.

"Yes, sir. I'm going to Hermann on the train."

Tobias didn't notice that everyone started paying attention to his conversation. Brother Curry asked, "Are you going with someone?"

"No, sir. It's just me. I'm going on an adventure."

Then several people began to ask questions like, "Have you done this before?' and "Have you been to Hermann?" and "Have you been on the train?" and "Do you know someone in Herman?"

Brother Curry asked, "Why Hermann?"

Tobias answered "Because they have good food in Hermann and they have good people in Hermann."

"Now I'm beginning to understand," Brother Curry smiled and said. "I'll bet this has something to do with bratwurst mit mustard."

Hermann

The next Sunday, Tobias put on his favorite clothes and went to the Mansion for his breakfast. The staff asked if he would like them to pack a lunch for his trip. "No thank you," he replied. Then he smiled and said, "I have plans for lunch."

The staff wouldn't accept his answer, however, and they handed him a small sack with a ham sandwich and an apple. Tobias went back to the barn and took a few dollars from his tin. He had no idea how much to take but he decided on five and thought that he could always put most of it back. Then he patted the Appaloosa and checked her food and water. Then he told her goodbye for the day.

The hill to the train station was so steep that he found himself trotting instead of walking down to the station. He waited for a short time and was watching the ferry ply the river when he was startled by the sound of a whistle. He looked up to see the eastbound train slowing for his stop. The adventure was beginning.

Tobias followed two other men to some small steps on the back of one of the railroad cars. A conductor was there asking to see tickets. The two men showed theirs and the conductor stepped to his left allowing them to go to the right into a passenger car. Tobias presented his ticket and the conductor punched it and stepped to his right leaving room for Tobias to go to his left and enter a different car. Much to Tobias's surprise, everyone in his railroad car was black like him.

He didn't think anything of it because he didn't know what to expect anyway. Tobias had grown up in a black community and the only white people he had known had been kind to him. Tobias had not yet experienced pains of racial bias and for today, he just accepted this as a part of his adventure and didn't even recognize the ugly implications.

As the train left the station and sped eastward, he realized that the people next to him were a family of four. The oldest girl was very talkative and wanted to know why Tobias was on the train. He explained that he was just wanting to see the world and maybe enjoy some good food. She said that her father's job had run out and they were on their way to St. Louis where he hoped to find work.

"Good luck with that, sir," Tobias said. Then he shuffled in his seat a little just to get more comfortable. When he did, he put his hand on the paper bag that the kitchen staff had given to him. He felt something hard inside so he peeked in to see what it was. He still couldn't tell so he took out the huge ham sandwich and the bright yellow apple and put them on the seat beside him. Then he saw in the bottom of the bag were two red and white peppermint candies. He thought about offering the candies to the children in the next seat and that's when he saw them starring at the sandwich.

Tobias thought for just a second and then asked, "Sir, do you have a sharp knife that I could borrow for just a minute?"

The father handed over a pocket knife which Tobias wiped and then used to cut the sandwich into four pieces. Then he cut the apple in half and divided each half again. "I just figured out what to do with this sandwich," he said. The cooks made this lunch for me but I have a sausage sandwich waiting for me in Hermann. Could you folks help me with this one?"

The oldest girl looked to her parents and then handed a sandwich piece to each of them and Tobias asked her to do the same with the apple pieces. He had been hungry enough times in his life to recognize what he saw as they tried to eat slowly and politely. The father of the family stood to reach across his children and shake Tobias's hand. He didn't need to say more. Tobias understood.

"Hermann!" the conductor called. "Arriving at Hermann."

Tobias nodded his head to the family and got up to leave. His paper bag was crumpled in the seat where he sat and he just left it there. Once off the train he looked back and saw them through the window and waved. He smiled to himself because he was being mysterious again. It was fun to have secrets.

The children scooted over into the seat where Tobias had been so they could stretch out a little more. The girl saw the crumpled bag and started to throw it away but she felt something rattling inside. She looked in to find two pieces of peppermint candy and two one dollar bills.

****

As Tobias stood on the railroad platform he looked up and down the main street of Hermann. It was the widest street that he had ever seen. He was surprised to see that almost every building was red brick or white stone. He didn't know where to begin. Then he saw the Holtgreve

Livery & Stable and knew that he could always talk to people about horses.

"Hello," Tobias said when he saw a man putting new shoes on a horse.

"Guten Morgen," the man replied.

"Do you speak English?" Tobias asked.

"Nein. Ich don's sprechen Englisch." The man replied then he called, "Karl!" and a boy slightly younger than Tobias came around the corner.

"Hi," the boy said. "What can we do for you?"

Tobias explained that he had never been to Hermann before and that he knew about the good food but wondered what else there was to see. The boy wasn't sure what to say. "How long will you be here?" he asked.

"Just until the westbound train comes through this afternoon."

"OK then, you might want to take the free trolley up to the Stone Hill Winery. The view up there is pretty special. Then you might want to just walk around town and see what stores there are. What kind of food do you like?"

"Bratwurst mit mustard," Tobias replied with a smile. Old Mr. Holtgreve, shoeing the horse, looked up when he heard that.

"OK then," the boy said. When you're ready to eat, go to that building with the white paint on the front. Tell them you want 'bratwurst mit senf.' They will ask if you want kraut. Be sure to say yes. They will bring you good potato salad with bacon like from the Deutschland. You will like it. And you won't want to eat again for two days!"

Tobias nodded his head to show that he understood. Then he said, "The farrier is very good. The horses trust him and he is very patient with them."

The boy smiled and said "You know horses!" Now they had something in common.

Without giving away his secret, Tobias said, "I almost live with horses. And I'm saving for one of my own."

The boys looked again at the farrier shoeing the horses. "I'm apprenticed to him." the younger boy explained. People all say he's the best but he's very hard to work for. He insists that everything be done perfect the first time. He's always telling me we don't have time to be doing things over."

Tobias remembered something his mother used to tell him. "If you don't have the time to do something right – where will you find the time to do it over?"

The younger boy said that was a great saying. He was going to tell it to his boss. When he did, the old man stopped what he was doing and came over to shake Tobias's hand. "Ich mag ihr denken," the man said.

The boy explained, "He likes the way you think." Then, pointing, he said, "Here comes your trolley."

****

What nobody else realized was that the important thing about Tobias's trip to Hermann was actually doing it all by himself. If he ever wanted to go out west he would have to travel great distances by himself and this was his first time to go anywhere alone.

He felt a thrill of walking through such a strange place and he thought he was the only black person there. Everyone else seemed to be German. That made it even more exciting. He loved his food that day and as he rode home on the train, the meal seemed to grow inside his belly. In his entire life he had never felt that stuffed feeling and he was afraid that something might be wrong.

It was dusk when he arrived in Jefferson City so he made his way up the hill to the barn. After checking on the horses, he fell asleep on a huge mound of straw.

Thirteen

Tobias awoke this morning in the Ledbetter bunkhouse and poured some water from the pitcher into the basin. He washed his hands and splashed some of the cool water on his face. The day was already warm – surprisingly warm for the 4th of September. Then he realized what he was just thinking and checked the big Ralston Feed Company calendar on the wall. Yes! Today was the 4th of September! Today Tobias was a teenager!

As he walked to the big table under the poplar tree for breakfast with the family and the other workers, he realized that he actually felt older. There seemed to Tobias to be a big difference between being twelve and being thirteen. He stood a little taller as he walked to the table that morning. It was nice to be here with these good people but it would also be nice to see Esther today. He would just like to tell her that he was thirteen now – just something he would like to share with her.

As he worked through the day, he counted his blessings. In the last eight months he had gone from being homeless and almost hopeless to having friends, a wonderful job, and soon – an Appaloosa of his own. Life was truly good. A birthday is a good milestone time to count your blessings and Tobias certainly felt blessed on this birthday.

Finished at Ledbetters

It was September 9 and the last Saturday before "books took up." School would start on Monday. That meant that it was Tobias's last day at the Ledbetter farm. It was Pay Day!

As usual, the work stopped early on Saturday afternoon and this time Tobias went with the other men to get paid. He was the last in line. When finally he stepped forward, Mr. Ledbetter said, "Well, Tobias, You've done some fine work and your pay has accumulated nicely. You have $47.25 to take home today!

Mr. Ledbetter handed the money to Tobias but Tobias looked puzzled. "I thought I would buy the Appaloosa and the saddle today, Mr. Ledbetter."

"Oh that," the farmer said. "I didn't think you were serious about that. What would you do with a horse?"

Tobias felt like someone had just kicked him in the gut. "Sir, I am serious and we had a bargain."

Mrs. Ledbetter stepped out of the house and said, "Tobias, don't you worry. This old fool tries to be funny but if people don't know him well, they don't understand his humor. We know how you feel about that horse."

Patrick chimed in, "Dad was teasing you, Tobias. Sometimes he does that. Sometimes he shouldn't."

"Hey, quit saying all these bad things about me," Mr. Ledbetter said. "Tobias, our deal was $45.00 for a horse and a fair saddle. If you still want to buy them, give me the money and we'll go to the barn so you can choose."

Tobias and all of the Ledbetters walked to the horse barn and Patrick asked, "Last chance to change your mind – Do you still want the Appaloosa?" Of course Tobias did.

Mr. Ledbetter said, "You can take any of these saddles. Now this one is the newest. This one is older but it's a better saddle. This one …."

Tobias interrupted and asked, "Can I have that one on the end?"

Mr. Ledbetter said, "Of course you may – but why that one?"

Tobias explained, "If I'm going to be a hand on a cattle ranch, I'll spend lots of time in the saddle and that one is the most comfortable. It also has the tallest sturdiest saddle horn for when I'm roping."

"Why am I not surprised?" Mrs. Ledbetter asked. "That's a very wise choice, Tobias."

Patrick was already busy helping with saddling the mare and Mrs. Ledbetter took one of Tobias's hands between her two hands and said that she hoped they wouldn't be strangers. "You're always welcome here," she said.

Mr. Ledbetter said, "Tobias you've seen me use this old pocket knife for a million chores. My father gave it to me when I was just about your age. This morning I gave one just like it to Patrick and now we want to give one just like it to you."

Patrick said, "You have to promise us now, every time you use your knife, you'll think about your friends on this farm."

Tobias put his left foot up into the stirrup and swung up onto his horse. He looked at the family and said, "I'll use the knife and I'll appreciate it but I'll never need anything to help me remember you. Thank you for everything."

School

School started on Monday. Tobias was sad to see that his previous teacher was gone. He had a new teacher who didn't smile the entire first day. She said her name was Miss Fitzsimmons but the boys immediately started calling her Miss Persimmons. Tobias didn't usually go in for calling people names but this one was funny because it really seemed to fit.

She gave them a morning recess and another one in the afternoon. She said that while the children played, she was working to keep everything "on track." One of the boys said, I'll bet anybody a penny that we won't get hot beans at lunch this year. On Wednesday, the third day of school, Miss Fitzsimmons called Tobias in from the afternoon recess. All of the kids in Tobias's class said things like "Uhm! Tobias is in trouble!" One of the boys said, "No, she's just calling him in because she's his girlfriend." The kids roared with laughter but Tobias just walked nervously toward the schoolhouse door.

When Tobias was inside, the teacher said, "I don't have much time so I'll just tell you that I want you to stay away from the Alden girl."

"Esther?" Tobias asked. "Why do I have to stay away from Esther?"

"Because she's a very attractive young lady and she's also very shy. You on the other hand are not shy. You're just full of stories that an impressionable young girl doesn't need to hear. The world has too many big-talking young men charming young women with their lies. Honestly, Tobias, do you think anyone believes that you have your own horse or that you're friends with the Governor? Just how stupid do you think we are?"

She reminded him to stay away from Esther and then sent him out of the building. In an unusual move for Tobias, he left the building, walked across the school yard and kept on going all the way home.

Paul saw him coming and could tell that something was terribly wrong. Tobias went into the barn and didn't come out so finally Paul went in. Tobias was standing next to his horse with his arms around her neck and crying. Paul could tell from his posture that these weren't just tears of sadness. They were tears of anger. It was a powerful emotion that pushed these tears out and Paul wasn't certain that he even wanted to go near Tobias right now.

Finally he walked up and very quietly said, "Tobias, I don't know what happened but if you need a friend, I'll be happy to listen."

He turned then and started to walk away. "She's terrible and mean!" Tobias shouted. Paul had never heard Tobias shout.

"Who's terrible and mean?"

"Miss Fitzsimmons. She won't let me talk to Esther because she said that I'm full of lies and that I don't have a horse and I don't know the Governor and that nobody believes anything I say."

Calmly, Paul said, "I'm going back to work outside and I want to think this over. Come on out when you feel like it and we'll talk."

Tobias made a point to go outside before Paul left for the day. He saw that Paul had a huge smile on his face when he said, "It will be hard for you to go to school tomorrow but it is important that you do. And if you will, I promise that you'll be happy that you did. As for Miss Fitzsimmons, don't say anything to her unless she asks you to. You just keep on being a good kid and tomorrow at this time, you'll be a happy kid – I promise."

Tobias didn't even ask Paul any questions. Remember, Tobias liked mysteries. He understood the value of a good secret. So the next morning, Tobias arrived at school on time and when the students went inside, Tobias went to his desk and tried to be as polite as he could. He thought about the strange expression on Paul's face and almost couldn't contain his curiosity about what Paul might be doing.

Then a movement outside the window caught his eye. He looked again and saw the team pulling the small carriage and Paul was driving. Mrs. Hadley was in the passenger seat. The carriage stopped right in front of the school door so everyone could see and the First Lady of the State stepped out.

Miss Fitzsimmons may not have known who the lady was but someone said, "It's Mrs. Hadley. It's the Governor's wife."

Mrs. Hadley, in one of her finest dresses, walked up to the front door and with all her charm and sweetness asked for Miss Fitzsimmons. Miss Fitzsimmons stepped forward and said, "That's me, ma'am."

"Oh, how nice to meet you," Mrs. Hadley said. "I have a note for Tobias. Will you please be sure that he sees it? I'll wait for his answer."

Miss Fitzsimmons took the paper to Tobias and glanced at it as she did. It was hand-written on the Governor's official stationery. It said,

"Tobias, my friend, may I please borrow your Appaloosa mare to go riding with some other fellows?

Sincerely,
Herbert S. Hadley"

Tobias read the note and smiled a huge smile. He turned to Mrs. Hadley and said, "Sure. Any old time."

The lady said, "Thank you, Tobias. This will mean so much to Herbert. Have a wonderful day!" Then she left and Tobias did have a truly wonderful day!

A Fine Proper Name

Tobias continued to go faithfully to school every day and the other students were truly impressed with the visit from the state's First Lady and his ownership of a horse. Tobias had never been a person to brag but Paul and the Hadleys had done it for him. He became very popular among his school friends for the first time ever.

Miss Fitzsimmons, however, seemed to think that Tobias had challenged her and shown her up. She was much more careful about what she said but she could find nothing about Tobias that she liked. In fact, she seemed to hate the sight of him in her classroom. Tobias continued to attend even though he was miserable.

The school superintendent announced one day that the schools would be closed on Friday, October 20th. The teachers were all required to attend an important meeting but the students would have the day off.

"I want to have another adventure," Tobias told Paul. "But this time I won't go on the train. I want to take my horse and ride to another town. I want to camp and sleep outside and live like a cowboy. There's no school on the 20th so I'll go to Sedalia that day and come back the next day."

Paul pointed out that Sedalia is sixty miles away and that's pretty far for a two-day trip. "Let's think about that for a while," he said. "Maybe a closer town would be better."

Later that day Governor Hadley came walking back from his temporary office and stopped to see how Paul and Tobias were doing. Paul told the Governor about Tobias's plan for a long trip in the saddle.

The Governor smiled and said it sounded like "an ambitious undertaking" but he also was concerned about the great distance in such a short time. Then he left for the Mansion and Paul and Tobias went back to work touching up the paint on the carriage's wheels.

That afternoon Paul saw one of the ladies from the kitchen waving to them. He went a little closer and she called as loud as she could. "Mr. Hadley wants to see you two. Both of you."

Paul and Tobias covered their paint cans and wrapped their brushes to keep them from drying out. They washed their hands and faces and then went straight to the Mansion. The Governor was sitting with two gentlemen at the large dining table. They each had a cup of coffee and a plate of tiny sandwiches sat in front of them.

"Here they are now," the Governor said. "Come on in gentlemen. Have a seat."

Paul looked down at his overalls and stood for a second but the Governor said, "Don't worry about those overalls. They're fine. Now, pull up a chair – both of you." Then he looked toward the kitchen. "Iris, come and see what Paul and Tobias might like to drink."

Then the Governor's voice became quieter and more businesslike. "Tobias," he said, "these men are friends of mine whom I recently appointed to the State Supreme Court. This is Justice Hart and the tall one there is Justice Bollinger. We were just visiting and I remembered our conversation earlier about your traveling long distances on that fine horse and well, we have some questions for you."

"A young man riding around the state on a beautiful animal like that might encounter some problems – especially a young black man. Did the Ledbetters give you a written title or bill of sale for the mare?"

Tobias answered, "Yes sir, it's in . . . It's where I keep my valuable things."

"And what name did they put down for you on that title?" the Governor wanted to know.

They put my name, sir – Tobias."

Justice Hart spoke then. "You see, son, that might be a problem since there is only one name on it. In legal matters it's really important to have both your first name and your last name – your family name. What is your father's last name?"

"I don't rightly know, sir."

"Times are different now than in the past, Tobias. Not long ago some people could do fine with just one name but that's not true any more. That's especially true for anyone wanting to own property."

Governor Hadley asked, "Tobias have you seen your father recently?"

Tobias explained that one day he had gone by to see his Pap and found someone else living in his house. Then he went to the tavern where his father would hang out and the men there said that Pap had moved away. Kansas City, they thought.

The Governor said, "I also asked someone to find your father and he brought back the same story. You father seems to have disappeared somewhere in the Kansas City area. I wanted to ask him about your last name but I don't think that's going to be possible."

Justice Hart spoke again, "If you're going to be a rancher and buying and selling horses and cattle and maybe even land, you definitely will need a full name. Since this is such an unusual circumstance we can file a motion for "Change of Proper Name" and take away any future legal problems.

"What would my name be?" Tobias asked nervously. Tobias is a good proper name isn't it?"

Judge Bollinger said, "I happen to know that Tobias is an old Hebrew name from the Bible. It means 'God is good' so that's a very proper name. But, Tobias, you have an opportunity here to choose your last name. It can be anything you like."

"Anything? Anything at all?" Tobias was getting into the spirit of having a true grown-up name. A real business name. A rancher's name. "Can I have a middle name too?" he wanted to know.

It was all smiles around the table when they told him that he could choose a full and proper name. A middle name and all. Judge Hart asked, "Would you like to think about some names and then come to my office some day? When you're ready I'll take care of the paperwork for you."

"Actually," Tobias said, "I've thought about this before. "If I could choose any name at all, I would like to be Tobias Paul Hadley."

All eyes turned to the Governor who seemed to be completely flabbergasted. Then he smiled and nodded his head. Judge Hart said, "That's a fine proper name." A woman's voice in the kitchen was heard to say, "That's a wonderful name."

Justice Hart told Tobias, "If you will bring the bill of sale for your horse, I'll take care of that too. We'll just make everything legal right here and now. Do you think another Supreme Court Justice and the Governor of Missouri will be good enough witnesses?"

Sedalia

September had turned to October and the first two weeks were almost over. There was a chill in the air and the Governor was always talking about something called football and when he did he sounded funny. He said things like Mizzoo-rah instead of the regular Missouri. He came from a game in Columbia one day talking about the Statue of Liberty play so Tobias figured that football must have something to do with plays and theaters.

Tobias asked Paul again about the trip he wanted to make to Sedalia. Paul still didn't think it was such a good idea. It was just too far and, if there was trouble, there wasn't anyone Tobias could turn to for help. Tobias said, "If things get really bad, I can always find an A.M.E. Church and the people will help. It's what they do."

That afternoon the Governor cut through the yard again and stopped by to see how Tobias Paul Hadley and his friend were doing. The Governor said he had a suggestion to help with the trip. "I have a friend in Sedalia," he said. "Now this man runs a saloon but he is a very good man. If I send a note introducing you, he will be very happy to help in any way he can. Not that I think you're going to need help – but just in case. I also feel that you should think about making this a three-day adventure instead of two. It's just too much for two days."

Tobias talked with Brother Curry and told him that he would be missing church on October 22nd and he told him why. Brother Curry said, "I truly envy you, Tobias. You get so much out of life! You make me wish I was young again."

The minister sat down at his desk and wrote a list on a piece of paper. "These are some A.M.E. Churches in Sedalia, Smithton, Tipton, California, and Otterville. If you get in any trouble, go to these people. If you're near one of these towns on Sunday morning, stop there for the service. They will make you welcome."

It was settled. Tobias was going all the way to Sedalia and back on his tall gray mare. He did his lessons at school but his mind was always on the adventure that awaited. In truth, school just wasn't fun anymore. He had always enjoyed the friends and the new things to be learned. He had always been challenged but he rose to meet the challenges and had almost always succeeded. Now everything was different. Miss Fitzsimmons had changed everything.

The morning of the 20th finally arrived. Tobias had been packing and preparing for days. He had a blanket roll tied behind his saddle. He had two feed bags hanging from under the bed roll. In the bags were some matches tightly wrapped in waxed paper, some food that the ladies in the kitchen had sent, the tin container with all his money, a change of clothing, and a hatchet for chopping firewood. In his pocket was the pocket knife that the Ledbetters had given him for occasions just such as this.

He left at dawn just before the sun was up. Paul wasn't at work yet and he wasn't sure that he saw the Hadleys but several people waved from the Mansion. Westward he rode on the gravel highway which paralleled the railroad. Soon he was riding beside the highway because the gravel was not good for the mare's hooves. After a time, however, the gravel which had been laid for automobiles ended and the road was dusty and dirty but was good for the horse.

As he rode, several trains passed and he didn't envy those passengers at all. He was much happier astride this beautiful animal with the autumn wind in his hair than he would be sitting on a mohair seat and looking out a window.

One lesson that Tobias learned on this trip was that being sure of oneself is not enough. He was so confident and proud that he didn't give enough consideration to the experience and knowledge of others. Paul and Governor Hadley had both expressed doubts about making this trip in two days. Tobias realized that they had always been right and he was not going to make it to Sedalia on that first day.

The wind was cold that night but he found a small outcropping of rock on a hillside. It was only about eight feet tall but that was enough to shield him from the wind. After he took care of his horse he built a small fire and settled for the night. He ate some jerky and some cornbread cakes that the ladies had given him.

He was surprised how cold the wind was. He expected the outdoors to be pretty much the same as sleeping in the barn. Here he even had a fire for warmth. Now he realized that the solid walls of the barn and the deep straw had been truly good. Tomorrow night he would look for a farmer's barn and ask if he could sleep there. He would also put on a second layer of clothing. This night he had to cover himself with the blanket, plus the horse blanket, and then a thick layer of dry leaves but he still shivered all through the long dark windy night. He kept asking himself, "Why didn't I bring my winter coat?"

The next morning, as soon as there was a tiny bit of light, he made his way to an oak tree back near the road and picked up all the fallen branches he could carry. He built up the fire and stood facing it and then tuned to warm his back side. It took a long time to chase away the shivers.

His horse was grazing but she seemed happy to feel the warm blanket and saddle. Maybe she was happy to be back on the road. Maybe she knew the exercise would warm her. Maybe she was a "free spirit" like Tobias and just enjoyed the adventure.

****

It was about 10:00 in the morning when Tobias arrived in Sedalia. He asked for directions to find John Silverton, the man recommended by Governor Hadley. It took almost an hour to find Mr. Silverton. He was at his saloon getting ready for the day's business. When Tobias walked in wearing his jeans with a belt and a plaid shirt he looked like a cowboy to Mr. Silverton. All he needed was some western boots.

Tobias looked around. One man was washing glasses behind the bar. That was probably Mr. Silverton. One man was cleaning and polishing the brass rails and trim. Another man was playing the piano. He wasn't exactly playing it – more like practicing it. Tobias thought the man must be trying out some new music.

As Tobias approached the man behind the bar the man was thinking, "If this kid tries to buy a drink, I'm gonna throw him so far out into that street…"

Instead Tobias said, "Good morning, sir. Are you Mr. Silverton?"

The man nodded that he was and Tobias continued, "My name is Tobias and I'm just traveling today but Governor Hadley said that I should come by and introduce myself. He said some really nice things about you."

"So you're a friend of Herbert Hadley, are you?"

"Yes, sir. I run errands for him and I help with his horses and carriages."

"Well, imagine that," the man said. "You know, being a saloon keeper, many people don't think I'm a proper person but Herbert knows that I have a good reputation and that I can get him votes when he needs them. I probably know more people around here than he knows in Jeff City." John Silverton paused for a minute and then said, "Herbert Hadley is a genuinely good person. He's the real thing. But I guess you know that don't you, son?"

Tobias was about to answer when there was a commotion behind him. He turned to see the piano player standing up and the piano bench had fallen over on the floor. In the door stood a black man with a round face and wearing a very nice suit of clothes.

John Silverton hurried from behind the bar and grabbed the man's hand to shake it. "My, my, my!" He said. "Look what the cat dragged in! They told me you were back in Missouri but I thought you were in St. Louis. My, my my! Didn't like life in New York I heard."

The man said, "Hello, John. Good to see you again." The piano player had come up to stand beside Mr. Singleton. The man looked at the piano player and said, "Hello, Pete. Is life being good to you?"

Tobias could see that this man was well-liked and he must be prosperous but there was something wrong with him. He seemed to be ill. There was something about the way he moved that wasn't right.

Mr. Singleton said, "So Scott, have a seat here and tell us what you've been doing. Are you back in Sedalia to stay? Fill us in."

The man began to fill in his friends on the past few years and Tobias listened to the fascinating tale. "To be honest," the man said, "I just got fed up with New York so I moved back to St. Louis. I just took the train over here today to talk to the people at Stark Publishing and to visit with old friends."

"As to your other question, I just finished a number called the Pine Apple Rag because that's what the public wants and that's what pays the bills while I do what I really like. I just finished an opera called Treemonisha. Now I'm trying to sell it to a producer."

"My, my, my!" John Singleton said again. Then he noticed Tobias standing and listening to everything. "Come over her quick, son. You have a chance to meet somebody pretty special. Scott Joplin this is … uh…"

"Tobias, sir. My name is Tobias Paul Hadley."

Scott Joplin said, "Grab a chair, Tobias. It's nice to meet you," and he reached out to shake Tobias's hand.

Tobias had no idea just who Scott Joplin was but he did of course understand that he wrote music and he must be famous. He soon learned what a magnificent piano player he was also. The other men begged him to sit at the piano for a minute and play his new Pine Apple Rag and then he played another one called The Maple Leaf Rag which he said was named for a business right there in Sedalia. Tobias noticed that as the man played his music, people began to come in off the sidewalk.

Mr. Silverton slapped his knee and said, "He can draw 'em in, this one can! He can just pull 'em in off the street!"

****

As Tobias left Sedalia that day and rode toward home he kept hearing the ragtime piano music in his head and he tried to sing it, "ta..ta..ta..ta..ta..ta..ta..tah,   ta..ta..ta..ta.   ta..ta..ta..ta..tah, ta..ta..ta..ta..ta..ta..tah,…" The appaloosa's ears would perk up at those times and Tobias thought, "She thinks I've gone completely crazy."

Tobias rode all day Saturday and was near California at a place called McGirk as the sun neared the horizon. There were no barns in sight so it looked like it would have to be another night sleeping outside. This time he allowed himself plenty of time to gather firewood. He looked more carefully for a good campsite. He found a rocky spot near a small creek where he and the horse could get fresh water. This place also had a little green grass surviving the October chill.

There was no wind tonight but Tobias wasn't taking any chances. He carefully built a fire on the rocks. There he noticed the remains of some previous fire. He felt good knowing that someone else had chosen this place. That must mean that he did a good job this time. Tobias also stacked a good amount of dead wood near the fire and near his bed roll so he could add wood as the night went on.

This night was much more comfortable and Tobias awoke the next morning in good spirits and looking forward to getting back home. He wondered if he would make it in time to attend church. After he left his campsite and was riding eastward into the warm morning sun, he realized that he was doing things without thinking about them. Certain things were becoming habits as he became more and more accustomed to having a horse for his partner and traveling from one unknown place to another. He felt like he was becoming truly independent.

11-11-11

Saturday, November 11, 1911 is a date known to every historian and meteorologist in the state. But, back then, people had no way of knowing what they were about to experience. The entire Midwest had been basking under a blanket of very warm air for several days now. Farmers were getting more work than usual done in their fields. Hunters, accustomed to shivering in their deer stands, were now soaking up the sun with their sleeves rolled up or even shirtless. Children were still splashing in local streams and coming home with fish or crawdads. In Jefferson City some people had gone back to their summertime practice of sleeping on their balconies.

On this Saturday Tobias saddled up his Appaloosa and took her for a ride. Even though he was only going to be gone for a few hours and would be back by sunset, he was still practicing for life on the open range and he took his pocket knife, his bedroll, and two empty feed bags as if they were saddle bags.

On this day he would go south toward Brazito. The sun was shining in a brilliant blue sky and the temperature was already in the seventies that morning. By noon the thermometer had already climbed to 80°! Tobias wondered how warm it might get today. He rolled up his sleeves as far as he could and rode with the hot sun on his back. Even though it was November, he wore his broad-brimmed straw hat and he was glad to have it keeping the hot sun off his head.

Just as he arrived at Brazito's little general store things began to happen. He immediately noticed people who were pointing at something behind him and were hurrying here and there. He turned to look back and saw what looked like someone had taken a black paint brush and painted a line across the horizon. Then a blast of cold air hit him in the face.

Trees began to bend as a fierce cold wind howled out of the north. If Tobias had stopped to think he would have taken refuge in someone's barn or in their house if invited. All he could think of, however, was the safety of home and friends. He wheeled and turned the mare's nose to the north. Trotting at first and then galloping they raced for the safety of the Governor's barn. Quickly Tobias realized that the horse would do whatever he told her but that she would die if she tried to gallop all the way home. He slowed her to a trot and they moved steadily and rapidly toward safety.

Tobias rolled his sleeves down and buttoned them but that was little help at all. He could tell that this was going to be a drastic situation. Now, in the distance, in that terrifying mass of dark clouds he could see lightning and he was riding straight into it. This wasn't like a summer storm though, and Tobias could tell that the cold was going to be at least as much of a problem as the wet.

Then he got what turned out to be a brilliant idea. He took the wool blanket that was his bedroll and opened it up. The horse pawed the ground nervously as he worked. She instinctively knew that danger was at hand. Tobias used his pocket knife and cut a twelve inch slit in the very middle of the blanket so he could put it over his head like a cape or a poncho. Then he did something which seemed a little silly at the time but it may have saved his life. He took the two empty feed bags and cut slits in the very bottom and in each side. He then slipped them both over his head and wore them as shirts.

Now wearing his shirt, two feed bags, and a wool blanket, he climbed back atop his strong horse. Tobias spread out the blanket like a tent so it covered a large part of her back and it also held her warmth inside for Tobias. Then he kicked her flanks and said, "Giddap old friend. Take me home."

Now the clouds in front of him were moving and it looked like they were boiling as lighting flashed everywhere in them. The first drops of rain hit Tobias in the face like someone was slapping him with cold wet hands. The drops were huge and they stung like stones. The thunder grew closer and closer and the lightning now kept the clouds active with lights that never stopped.

The black clouds seemed to be boiling and the thunder now was deafening. To be honest Tobias was not acting wisely at this point. He should have sought shelter somewhere but he was terrified and all he could think of was his dry barn.

As if to magnify his fear, hailstones began to bounce off his hat and his shoulders and his blanket. He turned his hat downward so he wouldn't be hit in the face but, even through the hat and the blanket, the huge hailstones pounded him like hammers. He could think of no way to protect his horse out here in the open and she couldn't wear a hat if he had one. He knew her well enough to know that she was about to balk. If she did stop on that open road, surrounded by open fields, they would both die.

Then, thankfully, the hail stopped. But it was replaced by sleet. The sleet was colder but it wouldn't beat you to death like the gigantic hailstones would. The temperature kept dropping and Tobias and his mare moved steadily toward safety. Tobias figured that the temperature must be near the freezing mark by now but – how could that be? "It must just seem that cold," he told himself. "It couldn't drop 50° in a couple of hours!" But this was sleet and you don't see sleet in warm weather.

The sleet only lasted for a short time – until the snow began to fall. When the flakes would land on the wool blanket, Tobias could see that they were big fluffy ones. The sky was completely covered with dark clouds now and lighting continued to flash violently as the snow fell. The scariest part of the snow was that it was carried on a howling wind. The cold north wind drove the snow so fiercely that Tobias began to have trouble seeing the road. A few times he couldn't even see the ears of his horse!

Tobias was lost. This was unfamiliar country to him. But he was certain that he was on the correct road. He thought that, if he saw a farmhouse, he would stop and ask for shelter but the heavy snow kept him from seeing almost anything. He didn't know it but, by this time, records show that the temperature had fallen to 9° and he was wet, cold, lost, and terrified.

Tobias saw something unusual between the road and a farmer's fence. Was it a tree trunk? Then he realized it must be a deer. He slowed his horse for a better look and saw that under the thick layer of snow was a man. Tobias jumped from his horse and rushed to the man.

It was a hunter. He was dressed in bib overalls with a thin shirt, no jacket and no hat. His body was already frozen stiff. Tobias didn't know what he might do for the poor man so he got back up in the saddle and continued his desperate journey. The memory of that stiff blue face haunted Tobias for years after.

In a short time the snow stopped and only the wind was reaching out for Tobias. It was the wind who wanted most fiercely to knock him off his saddle and leave him stiff in the snow for some stranger to find. He had beaten the rain, the hail, the sleet, and the snow. But now the wind was the final monster keeping him from safety. At one point the wind grabbed the wool blanket and pulled it up and back. It covered Tobias's face and tugged at his neck.

The monster used the blanket to try and pull him off his fine horse but Tobias clung tight to the saddle horn and stayed seated. "Damn you, wind!" he screamed. "You will not get me! "I'm Tobias Paul Hadley and you will not get me! Please, God in Heaven, help me!" he shouted. "Don't let me die out here!"

The struggle went on until finally the wind gave up and whimpered away to look for other victims and leaving only his partner, the cold. Then, on the horizon, Tobias saw a collection of rooftops and he knew it must be Jefferson City. The horse also seemed to know that safety was ahead. Perhaps she recognized the rooftops or, more likely, she smelled the smells of a warm city. At any rate, she perked up and took her partner home to the barn they shared.

Inside the barn, Tobias lavished the horse with attention. He broke the crust of ice from the water trough then covered every horse with blankets and fastened them tight. They each got a helping of oats with extra oats and a little molasses for the Appaloosa.

Just then the barn door opened and another lantern lighted the entrance. It was a housekeeper from the Mansion. "We're all having cocoa," she said, "and you're to join us." After two mugs of steaming cocoa and a roast beef sandwich, Tobias was told that he couldn't sleep in the barn that night. A cot had been prepared behind the kitchen.

****

The next morning Tobias went to church and they had a very special but very short service. It seems that many people had died all around the state the previous day. Worst hit were the hunters, often in the most remote areas and miles from home they were the most susceptible. But there were many others also. Automobiles had slid off the roads and crashed. Entire families on picnics, old people who just couldn't walk fast enough to reach safety. Many more were killed by lightning. The farmers' livestock and the wildlife were also hit hard and carcasses were everywhere. Some homes no longer had roofs. It had been a monster storm.

That morning they gave thanks for their safety but immediately began helping others. The usual Sunday noon meal was made into individual meals and taken to those in need. College students from Lincoln Institute came to offer their strong young backs and willing hands. Everywhere people bundled up tight and pitched in to help each other.

This all reminded Tobias of the aftermath of the great fire. Everyone helped each other and, together, everyone made it through. It's amazing what people become and what they can do after a disaster.

A New Trail

Tobias was affected drastically by his experience in the storm. He spent the following day, Sunday along with his church family helping others. He told the house staff that he didn't like sleeping on a cot and that he really preferred his own bed of straw so he went back to the barn. That night he was so exhausted that he fell asleep immediately. But he awoke many times dreaming of the cold and the wind and the stiff blue face.

The next morning he had managed to fall asleep again and Paul found him still sleeping under his layers of straw. It was late and Tobias chose not to go to school but instead went down to the riverfront. He watched in amazement as the Missouri River Bridge's huge main span swiveled and moved out of the way as a river boat glided through. Then it slowly swiveled back to become a road again for automobiles.

Tobias saw the automobiles streaming across the powerful bridge and wondered who was in there and what stories they might be able to tell him. He watched the ferry boat plying the river and saw the many kinds of people getting on and off. "How many other kinds of people are there?" he wondered. "I know the west has Indians and Chinese. It has mountains and wild horses. I know the cattle are different there. I wonder if they have bratwurst mit mustard. What other good things might they have?"

He was sitting there on that cold November day in the bright sun made even brighter by its reflection off the river when he made his momentous decision. "I'm going west," he said to himself. "I'm going out west today. "I'm going out west TODAY!"

Tobias moved with a happy determination up the hill to the Mansion's barn where he found Paul unloading bags of feed. Paul saw him coming and noted the joyous smile and turned to face the younger man. "Tobias," he said, "What lit you up today?"

Tobias spread his arms and threw his head back and said, "I'm going out west and I'm leaving today!"

He wasn't prepared for Paul's reaction. Paul asked Tobias to come back to his "office" and sit down. He said, "Tobias, I hate to see you leave school. I know you're miserable there this year but maybe we could find a different school for you. I just hate to see you quit school."

Tobias said, "I think that my mother would say the same thing but she never had the kind of dreams that I do. She was happy to stay in her home and make it nice. I want to see the world and meet new people and go places where nobody ever went before."

"Tobias," Paul said, "The Governor left on the train yesterday for Kansas City and some other places that were hit hard by the storm. He'll be stopping by here tomorrow before he leaves again for some other damaged places. Tobias, It will break his heart if you leave without telling him goodbye."

Tobias said, "I wouldn't want to go without seeing him either. If he'll be back tomorrow, I'll wait until then. That will give me more time to get ready."

Tobias decided to take the winter coat. It was too small but it was better than no coat at all. The straw hat was just a frazzled bunch of partially woven straw. It looked like it might have been a basket at one time. The hail had torn it to shreds. He took two empty feed bags and tied them together to make saddle bags and used harness polish on his shoes one last time.

All of his clothes didn't fill even one of the feed bags but he took overalls, shirts, long underwear, stockings, everything. He decided to wear the wool cap but when he got his first job he would get a real western-style hat and a pair of boots with riding heels. He was so much taller that he also would need a new pair of jeans as soon as he could afford to get some.

Tobias shined his saddle with saddle soap and cleaned its brass. He put oil on the wooden stirrups and more saddle soap on the reins. "You and I are going to be living outside," he told the Appaloosa. "No more comfy barns for us. You're gonna be a cow pony! But we're going to Texas where the weather is still warm."

By nightfall Tobias realized that taking the day to get packed and organized had been the right thing to do. Paul always knew the right thing to do. If a person listened to Paul they would always be OK. Tobias was really going to miss him. There would be many times in the future when Tobias would be in doubt and then ask himself, "What would Paul do?"

Tobias began looking back over his time in Jefferson City. Paul had been almost a father to him and Brother Curry had been like a wise and kind grandfather. Governor Hadley had been like an uncle but different. He was a powerful man with a mystique about him that set him apart. Already, in these young years, Tobias realized that the time he spent with Governor Hadley was something special to be treasured.

Paul arrived at work early the next morning because he knew that Tobias would be eager to begin his life's biggest adventure. When he came into the barn he saw the Appaloosa's saddle waiting and Tobias was coming from behind some hay bales with a tin container of some kind. He put that into his feed-bag-saddle-bags.

"I'm not sure those feed bags are going to hold up very well on a long journey," Paul said.

"I suppose I might have to get others if these give out," Tobias answered. "I'm not going to spend any of my money until I have a job to earn more."

"I understand," Paul replied, "but why don't you use these?" He reached around the corner and produced a beautiful new pair of leather saddle bags that matched Tobias's saddle. "I made these for you," Paul said, "because I knew you'd need them one day. I just hoped it wouldn't be so soon."

Tobias just stood there staring and speechless until Paul started taking things from the feed bags and putting them into the saddle bags. Tobias stepped in front of Paul and gave him a huge hug. They slapped each other's backs as they hugged and then went back to work without saying anything.

When it was finally 8:00 Paul said, "You know the Governor was supposed to come in on the train this morning but he was so bushed that he came on last night's train instead. I'm sure he's up and around by now. Let's go and see."

They went in the west door of the Mansion and the lady with the gray hair clapped her hands three times which brought the entire kitchen staff. "We will miss seeing you around here at breakfast time, Tobias.

We will miss you so very much. We want to give you something to make your journey better."

One of the younger women handed her a small package which she handed to Tobias. This is for those times at night when you're all alone or it's just you and the cattle. We thought a guitar was way too big to carry.

Tobias untied the string and found a harmonica and a small book of instructions. It's just the right size for a saddle bag," he said. "I hope I can learn to play it. If I do, I'll come back some day and play The Maple Leaf Rag."

Just then everyone stepped back because they heard the Governor coming. He peeked into the kitchen and motioned for Tobias and Paul to join him in the dining room. As Tobias walked toward the dining room all of the ladies patted him on the shoulders and wished him "good fortune," and "God speed," and a "safe trip."

The Governor and Mrs. Hadley were waiting in the dining room when Tobias entered with Paul close behind. The Governor spoke first. "Your shoes look nice today, Tobias, if you were going to church. But we're a little worried about your being on horseback with that kind of a heel. I think these might suit your purpose to a better degree." He always talked like that but Tobias was used to it.

Mrs. Hadley stepped forward with a pair of tall boots with riding heels. They had a picture of a steer with long horns stamped into the leather. They were a beautiful brown color with a pointed toe.

Tobias took them and, with tears in his eyes, he looked them over from top to bottom and from heel to toe. "Those pointy toes help you get them into the stirrup easily. Now just wear them for a short time at first so they don't make sores on your feet."

"Will you listen to him?!" Mrs. Hadley said. "Always giving orders! He's just blustering to cover up how he feels."

The Governor smiled and said, "She's right, you know. She always is. Things are not going to be the same without you, Tobias. We will miss you deeply." He took Tobias's hand to shake it but then pulled him close to give him a hug. Then Mrs. Hadley gave him a hug also and they all walked him to the front door. "Be sure to stop at your church this morning," she told him. Reverend Curry would be crushed if you didn't see him on your way."

"The next time you come here, Tobias, don't come to the employee's door. You come through this front door as an honored guest. Do you understand?"

"Thank you, sir," Tobias said as he and Paul walked between the columns and down the steps. They walked past the fish pool which would someday hold a fountain featuring the statue of Tobias as a youth.

While Tobias slipped into his new boots, Paul tied the shoestrings together on his old shoes and hung them between the saddle and the bed roll. Then he led the Appaloosa out of the barn and Tobias tucked his harmonica and instruction book into a saddle bag. He tucked the string from the package in there also. "You never know when you might need something," he told Paul.

"Smart man," Paul replied. "Waste not – want not."

Tobias swung up into the saddle and reached down to shake Paul's hand one more time. "You're the best, Paul. Thank you for everything!" With that he headed the mare south toward the Quinn Chapel.

Brother Curry was sitting on the front steps in the sunshine arranging some papers. "Tobias!" he called. "I hoped I might see you before you left. The folks at church have a little something for you. You know we can't afford much because we have so many people in need after the storm. But we want you to have these things for your life's journey."

He handed Tobias a tiny book. "Just the right size for a saddle bag," Tobias thought. He looked at the book and realized it was a very small version of the New Testament.

"The answers to life's big questions," Brother Curry said in his best minister's voice. "That other thing is just to give you a good start."

Tobias looked in the little bag and saw a sandwich, an apple, and a small box with a piece of apple pie. He smiled and said, "The people here have already given me a good start. Tell them I said so. Tell them I said 'thank you'."

"Where will you go, Tobias?"

"I don't rightly know," was the answer. "First I'll go to Tipton and then I'll turn southwest toward Texas. You know Stephen Austin took a lot of Missourians there already. I'll just follow them and see what happens."

Tobias put his new boot into the stirrup and swung his right leg up and over the beautiful horse. He pulled the reins to the right and nudged her westward and out of town. From one hill he did look back. Everything he knew was there but not completely left behind. The memories, he took with him. But, in a very real way, all of the things he had known remained behind him and everything still to learn lay ahead.

Epilogue

Tobias wrote a few letters to Governor Hadley but he never knew what address to put on them. Once the Governor's term was up, he left Jefferson City and Tobias had no way to find out about him. The only letter that ever found its way to Mr. Hadley explained that Tobias had left Texas and was on a ranch near Silver City, New Mexico. He was doing well and was working for a cattle rancher that he really liked.

Tobias told the Hadleys that he had met a beautiful young Navaho woman. He described her dark eyes and long shiny black hair. She was in college at New Mexico Normal School and learning to be a teacher.

Paul went back to Jackson County where he got busy with the life he had been living before his time in Jefferson City. He had many children and grandchildren but he still thought of Tobias from time to time and wondered if his dreams were coming true.

Governor Hadley went on to become the Chancellor of Washington University in St. Louis. He founded the George Warren Brown Department of Social Work which became one of the best social-work programs in the United States. In his new job he saw many bright young men and women who were on their way to doing wonderful things but he always had a special place in his heart for a young boy he had known back in Jefferson City.

Sometimes when the day was over and the big city was growing quiet again, old Professor Hadley would enjoy remembering pleasant summer afternoons sitting in the shade of a horse barn. He loved to remember conversations with one old friend and one young friend. "Oh, Tobias," he would whisper. "What has become of you? I hope you're well, my friend."

Author's Note

Of course this story is historical fiction which indicates that it is a story made up by this writer but it is based on real people and real events. All we know for sure about our story's hero is a note that Agnes Hadley left about "…a little colored boy whom we found from time to time sleeping in the barn."

But history gives us tools to deduce what most probably happened in any given time or place. For instance there really was a lightning storm which set the Capitol Building on fire on February 5, 1911. Being only one block away, we can be fairly certain that any healthy boy would make his way over to see the spectacle and get drafted into working at the scene.

The Capital Building, Feb. 5, 1911

We also know that the fire brigade from the prison responded to the fire call and that they performed heroically. They were given great recognition in the days following the fire. And, yes, there were firemen who rode the train from Sedalia and brought their horses and equipment with them.

After the great fire the State Legislature really did meet in the second floor library at St. Peter's School. Because of this, the school can claim to be "the Ninth Capitol of Missouri."

In this story I have described Tobias's love of the people at the African Methodist Episcopal (A.M.E.) Church and how they served the community. The A.M.E. Church in Jefferson City is called the Quinn Chapel and it has truly been serving the city for over 160 years. In 1911 it was located just five blocks down the hill from the Governor's Mansion on the street that is now Highway 63 and Highway 50. The Central Bank's drive-through facility is now at that exact spot.

Cathay Williams was a real person who lived near Jefferson City. When she was "liberated" by the Union Army she was classified as "collateral" and forced to work for the army for the duration of the war. She washed their clothes, cooked their meals, tended their fires or whatever other chores might arise. At war's end, she knew only field labor and military life. She and her female cousin chose more of the military life. The two women enrolled at Jefferson Barracks in St. Louis for the cavalry unit of black troops who distinguished themselves in service and whom the Indians called "Buffalo Soldiers." For this period of time Cathay Williams called herself William Cathy.

Cathay Williams

We know what the schools were serving for lunch and that people in positions of power were trying to make the lunches better. We know that 1600 people gathered to pressure the road commission on August 2 of that year. (It's interesting to note that the commissioners must have had trouble choosing because we ended up with Highway 40 on the north side of the Missouri River and Highway 50 on the south side.)

It's quite likely that Tobias would have seen a ball game or two when the Senators were in town. Missouri had many minor league teams over the years including Hannibal's Cannibals. In 1911 the state's minor league and semi-pro teams included those Senators and Cannibals, the Brookfield Hustlers, the Kirksville Osteopaths, the Macon Athletics, the

Monett Athletics, the Sedalia Cubs, the Maryville Comets, the Joplin Miners, and a team from Carthage which was just known as Carthage.

The trolley car discussed in this story was the pride of Jefferson City. Trolleys were something brand new and were a great way to get around town in 1911. The streets were a lot cleaner after the electric trolley went by than after teams of horses went by.

A Jefferson City Trolley

If this young boy could live by himself we can be sure that he was a bright, and independent person, capable of taking care of himself even at a young age. There were no adults living with him so he must have been an orphan or somehow left homeless and on his own.

History shows us that Scott Joplin became fed up with New York in 1910 and moved back to St. Louis. We also know that he was in the early stages of a fatal disease at that time.

Of course the Orphan Train movement was underway from about 1855 to about 1930 and it did bring more than 150,000 children from the slums of eastern cities to new lives in the rural areas and small towns of the Midwest.

An Orphan Train

The events of November 11, 1911 are well-documented and thousands of unsuspecting people were caught in the nightmare storm that day. There were many tragic fatalities recorded.

We know that Governor Hadley was a powerful and compassionate man. This leader and politician spent only one term in office and then went on to found a very prestigious School of Social Work in St. Louis. He was deeply involved in a life of helping others less fortunate.

Herbert S. Hadley

These and many other details of the story are accurate. Other details are from the writer's imagination. This is how historical fiction can help us to understand the things that happened before our time. Would we otherwise be able to identify with a child whose entire existence is reduced to one sentence written by a woman who happened to encounter him "from time to time"?

One member of the Education Committee at the Governor's Mansion pointed out that Tobias probably wouldn't have thought about being a teen-ager. She explains that the notion of being a teen-ager didn't come into our society until the 1940s. Those in the age group of Tobias would just be called "young people" and at about fourteen or fifteen they would be called adults.

Today's youth will scoff at the idea of a thirteen-year-old leaving to become a self-supporting adult. But they should remember two things. The first is that, in times past, many young men left school and went to work at thirteen or younger. Many young women would be engaged to marry by age twelve. Many teachers had only recently graduated from eighth grade themselves. Times were very different. The second thing is that Tobias had been living on his own for a good deal of time before he went west so being self-supporting was nothing new to him.

The first bridge across the river at Jefferson City really did swivel to get out of the way of riverboats. It was so low that the boats could not squeeze underneath without breaking off their smokestacks. In the picture the tallest part of the structure is the part that was moved by a gasoline-powered then a diesel engine. It was on the south side of the river near the capitol building. Imagine being on a horse or driving cattle across the bridge when that began to move!

The Bridge at Jefferson City in 1911

Each year thousands of students on field trips and other visitors tour the grand old Governor's Mansion. As they wait their turn they often sit on the edge of what used to be a goldfish pool and they dip their fingers into the cool waters flowing from a bronze fountain called "The Children's Fountain."

Two of the children depicted in the fountain are Carrie Allen Crittenden who died of diphtheria while living at the Mansion. Another child is a grandson of the late Governor Mel Carnahan and Mrs. Jean Carnahan who was responsible for having the fountain created. Carrie Crittenden is there representing a hope for good health for our children. The Carnahan's grandson is representing the hope for a good environment for all living things in our state.

The African-American child we see in bronze is our Tobias. Of course he is depicted as the same age as the other children. He is shown reaching out to capture the water. The sculptor, Jamie Anderson, has said that this represents him reaching out to capture opportunity.

Reaching for Opportunity

Contributors

This writer wishes to thank the Docents at Missouri's Governor's Mansion and members of their Education Committee who have helped to make this story complete and to enhance its richness. They have given their time to read and comment on various aspects of the story. Because of these people, Tobias comes to life in a way that would not be possible without their help.

Other books in this series to be published in 2014 include:

The Monett Nine – Planes, Trains, Baseball Games, and the fascinating story of dealing with tragedy and living life for a boy in his small Ozarks town of long ago.

The Intrepid – Follow the adventures of a young boy as he serves as the Pilot's Apprentice on a steamboat. He meets colorful people as he works up and down the great rivers.

Boys of the 1800s – Five short stories about interesting boys from early Missouri.

* Boy who Dreams was an Osage Indian boy with special talents.
* Luc Gamache lived in St. Louis when it was very young.
* Ben and Silas were two boys in the frontier settlement of Arrow Rock.
* Matthew and Levi explored Westport before it was part of Kansas City.
* Timmy Moran came to Missouri from Ireland while his father was building the railroad from Hannibal to St. Joseph.

More Good Books
For Young Readers

SCHOOL EDITION
TALES FROM MISSOURI AND THE HEARTLAND
100 FOUR MINUTE STORIES

Here's that unique book of short stories. It will be used and appreciated for years!

Each story is followed by open-ended questions and discussion starters.

Eight Tough Kids

Stories to give and share with any 10- to 14-year old.

**These regular kids handle life's tough problems.
Tough times don't last but tough Missouri kids do!**

Forward by Cathy Westbury, Missouri's State Counselor of the Year

Look for Ross Malone's newest book,

Mysterious Missouri.
"Show-Me" the Strange Stuff!

**Monsters – Hauntings –
Strange Phenomenon –
The Unexplained
Some Weird – Some Funny – All True**

To order any Tales From Missouri Books: See the following page and visit www.RossMalone.com or www.Missouri☐ Books.com. Send the books marked below:

Name _____

Address _____

City, State, Zip _____

School Edition
Tales From Missouri and the Heartland, number of paperbacks _____

School Edition
Tales From Missouri and the Heartland, number of hard covers _____

Eight Tough Kids (available in hard cover books only) _____

Tobias and the Governor, number of paperbacks _____

Tobias and the Governor, number of hard covers _____

Total number of paperback books _____ X $17.00 = $_____

Total number of hard cover books _____ X $22.00 = $_____

Total number of books _____ X $3.00 Shipping & Handling = $_____

Total enclosed $_____

Thank you! Please make your check payable to "Tales from Missouri" and send the order to:

Tales From Missouri
1487 Clearview Road
Union, MO 63084-3032

Watch for these and other books at **www.RossMalone.com** or **www.Missouri—Books.com.**